"Tonight...at your house."

This would be the first time Sophie would get to explore Tommy's bed, his sheets, his pillows, his body.

That hot, hot body.

"Do you want to go out first?" he asked.

She cleared her mind. "I'm sorry. What?"

"You know, dinner and dancing."

Ohmygod. "Like a date?" She shook her head, even if he couldn't see her. "That isn't what this is about."

"We can skip it if you're not up for it." He paused. "I don't want you to be nervous, Soph."

Too late. She already was. "I'm trying to relax."

"I can't wait to be inside you." He spoke in a hushed tone. "It's all I've been thinking about."

He was taking control and sweeping her along, determined to start their affair with a romantic bang.

* * *

Nashville Rebel is part of the
Sons of Country series
from Sheri WhiteFeather.

Dear Reader,

I have a thing for bad boys. Maybe not so much in real life, but I'm fascinated with bad boy celebrities, which is why I created Tommy Talbot. He's the hero of this story and has been deemed "the baddest boy of country." I had fun redeeming Tommy and taming him. But while he was being bad, he was a lot of fun, too. His best friend is Sophie Cardinale. She's the heroine of this book and knows Tommy better than anyone. They grew up together, and now she works as his road manager.

But Sophie wants to get off the road and have a child, and Tommy just might be the guy to help her make that happen. Because, really, what's sexier than a former bad boy with a baby?

Love and hugs,

Sheri WhiteFeather

SHERI WHITEFEATHER

NASHVILLE REBEL

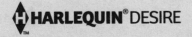

HARLEQUIN® DESIRE

Recycling programs
for this product may
not exist in your area.

ISBN-13: 978-1-335-97194-4

Nashville Rebel

Printed in U.S.A.

Sheri WhiteFeather is an award-winning, bestselling author. She lives in Southern California and enjoys shopping in vintage stores and visiting art galleries and museums. She is known for incorporating Native American elements into her books and has two grown children who are tribally enrolled members of the Muscogee Creek Nation. Visit her website at www.sheriwhitefeather.com.

Books by Sheri WhiteFeather

Harlequin Desire

Billionaire Brothers Club

Waking Up with the Boss
Single Mom, Billionaire Boss
Paper Wedding, Best Friend Bride

Sons of Country

Wrangling the Rich Rancher
Nashville Rebel

Visit her Author Profile page at Harlequin.com, or sheriwhitefeather.com, for more titles.

One

Sophie Cardinale couldn't do it anymore.

She couldn't be Tommy Talbot's tour manager, living her life on the road with nothing except the sound of Tommy's music roaring in her ears. She needed to put down roots, to get a desk job, to have a baby. At thirty-four, her biological clock wasn't just ticking; it was on the verge of exploding. She'd been thinking about this for the past year, day in and day out. It *never, ever* left her mind. But she hadn't told Tommy yet. He wasn't just her gorgeous, wild, pain-in-the-ass boss; he was also her closest and dearest childhood friend.

Sophie's father had worked for Kirby Talbot, Tommy's country-music-legend dad. Her dad had been Kirby's guitar tech up until the day he'd passed away, a little over two years ago. Sophie had never known her mom. She'd developed postpartum pre-eclampsia a month after she'd given birth to Sophie and had died as a result. Mom had been the love of Dad's life. He'd talked about her all the time, reminiscing about how sweet and beautiful she was. Her parents had met on the road, in the mid-1970s, when turquoise jewelry and leather vests reigned supreme. At the time, Mom worked for Kirby Talbot, too, as his wardrobe mistress. They got married, and Sophie had been born a decade later. Kirby had adored both of her folks. They were like family to him.

In fact, after Mom died, Sophie, her dad and her granddad, who'd also helped raise her, lived in one of the guesthouses on the Talbot family compound. That was how she'd gotten to know Tommy so well. According to his mother, they'd bonded as babies when she used to "borrow" Sophie to keep him company in his playpen. But mostly Sophie thought that Tommy's mom just felt sorry for her since she didn't have a mom of her own.

During their adolescence, Sophie and Tommy were inseparable, spending their time jumping out of trees, riding green broke horses and speeding around on his dirt bikes together. In those days, Sophie had been a pixie-haired, doe-eyed tomboy who'd had a crush on Tommy, and did almost anything he dared her to do. But she'd calmed down since then. Tommy? Not so much. He was still a daredevil, especially on stage.

Tommy trained with some of the best stuntmen

in the business. His most recent act involved riding a mechanical bull on a rising platform. He even stood up and danced on the bull to the opening riff of "Rebel with a Country Cause," one of his most popular songs. During his dance, the floor below him would erupt into flames.

His stunts weren't always planned or practiced. If he wanted to climb lighting trusses or do backflips into the crowd or douse his guitar with lighter fluid and set it on fire, he merely took it upon himself to do so.

On this latest tour, the one that had just ended, the pyrotechnics guys kept threatening to quit if Tommy didn't follow the rules. But it wasn't Tommy who had to suffer the wrath of the road crew. It was Sophie. Everyone took their complaints to her, expecting her to keep Tommy in line.

In the beginning, working for him had been exciting. She used to get a dangerous thrill out of it. Now, all these years later, she just wanted some peace and quiet.

But mostly she longed to become a mom. She'd already been checking out sperm banks, and soon she would be ready to concentrate on choosing a donor. Sophie had a bad track record with men. She'd given up on finding the right guy, and by now she needed some emotional security in her life. For her, becoming a single mom was the answer, even if it meant quitting her job and finding a new one in order to do it.

So here she was, behind the wheel of her truck,

driving to Tommy's ranch, to give him her notice. Sophie lived outside of Nashville, in the same area as Tommy. She had a modest home on a mini ranch, with two horses and two dogs, all of which she boarded at Tommy's place when she traveled with him. His spread was huge, boasting a custom-built mansion and a slew of ranch hands and caretakers. By now, Tommy was as rich and famous as his legendary father. Maybe even more so. Whereas Kirby Talbot had been deemed "the bad boy of country," Tommy had become known as the "the baddest boy of country," surpassing his dad in that regard. Mostly Tommy had earned that reputation because of how reckless he was on stage. But him being such a ladies' man was a factor, too, which had never sat well with Sophie.

As she approached the private road that led to Tommy's estate, she sighed in relief. Thankfully there weren't any fans at the gate, clamoring to see him coming or going on this September afternoon.

She buzzed the intercom and announced her arrival, and his security chief let her through. She'd already texted Tommy and told him to expect her. But she hadn't revealed the nature of their meeting or what it would entail. It wasn't going to be easy—of that she was certain. Tommy wasn't going to want her to quit. He wouldn't be happy about the reason she was quitting, either. Babies had become an anxiety-ridden subject with him. Earlier this year a woman named Kara Smith, with whom he'd had a one-night stand, claimed that he might be the father of her unborn child. He wasn't, as it turned out. Tommy was extremely careful about practicing safe sex. But the possibility that the protection could have failed still scared him and had taken an emotional toll on his bachelor, happy-go-lucky lifestyle.

After Sophie parked in the circular driveway, she exited her vehicle and smoothed the front of her tank top over her flat stomach. Hopefully a few months from now, she would have a cute little baby bump.

She rang the bell, and Dottie, the woman who ran Tommy's house, answered the door. She was the nicest lady, a grandmotherly type, who fussed over Tommy as if he was her own. But she wasn't a pushover, either. When the pigheaded superstar needed a tongue-lashing, Dottie was more than willing to do it, even if her reprimands didn't make a bit of difference.

"Hi, Dot." Sophie entered the colorfully tiled foyer. "Will you let Tommy know I'm here?"

"He's already waiting for you by the pool." When Dottie smiled, her friendly blue eyes crinkled beneath her glasses. Her salt-and-pepper hair was fixed in its usual short-and-simple style.

Sophie had a mass of long, wavy brown locks that never behaved. She was considering cutting it. Not now, but maybe after the baby was born. The baby she hadn't even conceived yet, she reminded herself. She needed to hurry up and plant that seed.

"Do you want me to bring you something cool to drink?" Dottie asked. "Or some lunch, perhaps?

Chef already has chicken salad with cranberries and walnuts ready to go."

"Thanks, but I'm fine. I don't need anything, except to talk to Tommy. I'll just go see him now."

She headed for the backyard, with its gigantic, lagoon-style grotto pool. Beneath the center waterfall was a waterproof cave, which had an entertainment room with rock walls, stone floors and a glamorous sitting area, complete with a spectacular sound system, a big-screen TV and a tiki-type bar. Tommy had built that room for his guests. For himself, he'd created a private apartment, accessible from yet another waterfall, for when he wanted to be completely alone and relax beneath his pool. No one except him had ever been inside it. He didn't even take his lovers there.

She saw him lounging in the sun, listening to music on a portable device, the earbuds planted firmly in place. His eyes were closed, and his light brown hair was still damp from a recent swim.

She was lucky that he was wearing trunks. Tommy had no qualms about nudity, and skinny-dipping was one of his favorite pastimes. Tempting as he was, whenever he stripped down in front of her, she tried to avert her gaze from the parts that mattered. She also made darn sure that he'd never seen her naked. Even when they were kids and splashing around in the stream on his daddy's property, she'd never peeled off her swimsuit in front of him—no matter how often he baited her to do it.

Sometimes he still baited her to get naked with him. And not just for swimming. Thing was, Tommy had been trying to hook up with her since high school. Yet even during their teenage years, he had too many other girls around him. After they graduated, Sophie had gone to college, while he focused on his music and gained notoriety. She'd earned a business degree and started working for him. She'd never considered the boss/employee aspect of their relationship a problem. In her own sinful way, she thrived on his playful flirtations. But since she was supposed to be the voice of reason, she made sure that he knew her boundaries. Nonetheless, she also fantasized about having a ridiculously steamy affair with him. Of course, that didn't mean she was going to act on those feelings. Her concern was his inability to settle down.

Tommy used sex like a weapon, a gun he never quit firing. Mostly he partook of groupies. On occasion, he had regular girlfriends, too. But he never made commitments to any of them. Brunettes, blondes, redheads: they were all his playthings.

Not this brunette, she reminded herself. She wasn't going to share his bed, no matter how exciting the experience might be.

Suddenly, he opened his eyes and stared straight at her. Funny how he sensed her presence at the very moment her mind was immersed in sex.

Sophie squinted at him, and he smiled. He had a lopsided grin that made him look like the troublemaker he was. Only his wildness wasn't fueled by anything except his hot-blooded nature. Although he threw some extravagant parties, Tommy never drank alcohol. He didn't do drugs, either. His father was a recovering alcoholic and addict, and Tommy vowed to never be like him, at least not in that regard.

She moved closer. The drink holder in the chair's armrest held his beverage of choice: a bottle of berry-flavored sparkling water. When he was on the road, she made sure that his hotels, dressing rooms, tour buses and private jet were all stocked with it.

He removed the earbuds. "Hey, Sophie-Trophy," he said, using one of the many nicknames he'd given her. Anything that rhymed, he used. Mostly he had to make up words. There weren't a lot that rhymed with Sophie or Soph. Or even Sophia, for that matter.

She sat in the chaise longue next to him and greeted him with a simple "Hello."

Idiot that she was, she stole a glance at his navel and the line of hair that disappeared into the waistband of his trunks. If he'd been naked, she never would have dared to look that low on his body. But for now, she took her fill. Or thrill. Or whatever.

Luckily, she'd worn shorts and sandals today. She didn't feel out of place sitting by the pool. But that didn't make her any less nervous about revealing her agenda.

Before she got the chance to start the conversation and spin it her way, he said, "I hope you came by to talk about extending the tour. I know it's supposed to be over, but I was thinking we could add more dates." He frowned into the sun. "I'm already going bonkers sitting around here and we've only been back for a few days."

She frowned, too. Not at the sun, but at him. "I know how stir-crazy you get when you're not on the road, but adding more dates is the last thing I've been thinking about."

He grabbed his water and took a swig. After he swallowed a noisy gulp, he asked, "So what's the deal, then? Why did you call this meeting? Am I in trouble? Is the insurance company threatening to raise my rates again?"

"No, it's nothing like that." She steadied her voice. But then she got antsy and just blurted it out. "I'm giving you my notice. I'm quitting so I can get a job with regular hours and less travel and have a baby."

If the pavement had just opened up and swallowed him whole, he wouldn't have looked more surprised. "Damn, really? You're pregnant? By who?"

He sounded offended. Or annoyed. Or frustrated. But he always acted that way when she was dating someone. As reliant as he'd become on her, he got jealous when she gave her attention to someone else. So much so that he tended to butt heads with her lovers. Not that she'd had many men. She'd never been in a relationship that was worth a damn. Her last boyfriend, a record exec, had cheated on her with his twenty-something assistant.

"I'm not pregnant yet," she replied. "But I plan to be."

A muscle tightened in his jaw. "Did you and Cliff get back together? Are you going to marry that jerk?"

She shook her head. "Are you kidding? I'd never get back with him, not after the way he betrayed me. I'm not planning on having my baby with anyone. I'm going to be a single mom."

He had a confused expression. "The last time I checked, it takes two to make a baby."

Sophie rolled her eyes. "I'm going to use a sperm bank."

"You're picking the guy out of a genetic lineup? Come on, Soph. That's crazy." He frowned again. "Besides, when did you get so maternal? I never knew you wanted kids."

"I've been thinking about it for a while now. And at my age, I can't wait forever. The older a woman gets, the more steps she needs to take to ensure a healthy pregnancy."

Tommy sat a bit more upright. "Have you cleared this with your doctor? You're not at risk for what your mom had, are you?"

"There could be hereditary issues, but they can't predict whether it would happen to me. Either way, my doctor assured me that they would closely monitor me for any signs of a problem. My mother didn't report her symptoms when they first appeared. She wasn't aware of how serious it was."

"Yeah, but still. Maybe you should just forget the whole thing."

"I can't." She craved the wonderment of being a mom. It was especially important since she'd never known her mother, and with her dad being gone a few years now, she missed having a family. Her grandpa had passed away a while ago, too. Sophie was all alone. "I'll never feel complete if I don't do this."

He winced. "So you're determined to go through with it?"

"Most definitely." She wasn't giving this up for anything. "I haven't put any feelers out there for another job. I wanted to give you my notice first. But I know enough people in this industry to find something suitable."

"You don't have to stop working for me. I can get you set up in the management office. You can join Barbara's team. I'm sure she would be happy to have you on board. She's always singing your praises, going on about how you're the only person who's truly capable of handling me."

"I certainly try." As for Barbara, she was his business manager, and the poor woman had her work cut out for her, trying to get Tommy to follow her advice. But she stuck by him, was loyal to the core. Of course, Tommy had offered Barbara a lucrative deal to represent him, making him her one and only client.

"Are you interested?" he asked.

"Yes, actually, I am." She would rather stay with his organization than start over somewhere new. But she had certain conditions if she was going to remain with him. "I'll call Barbara and arrange a meeting with her. But I want the same pay and the same benefits I have now, with Monday-through-Friday hours. No overtime, no mandatory weekends and no gigs. I'm not attending any of your shows, not even the local ones."

"Yeah, right," he scoffed. "You say that now, but I know what a workaholic you are."

"I mean it, Tommy. I'm not going to babysit you anymore."

"All right, all right." He held up his hands, Old West style, as if she was preparing to shoot him. "You can have whatever you want." He lowered his hands. "I just don't want you to go off and start working for someone else. It's going to be tough to replace you, as it is. I need you, Soph."

His words sent a jolt of heat through her veins. Damn, she hated it when he had that effect on her.

He raised his water bottle in a mock toast, his hazel eyes locking onto hers. "You're my go-to girl."

She forced herself to hold his gaze. The unwelcome heat was still attacking her body, but glancing away would be admitting defeat. She didn't want him to know he was making her weak.

"You mean 'woman,'" she said.

"What?"

"Go-to woman. I haven't been a girl since you put that rubber snake down the front of my shirt."

He burst into a reminiscent laugh. "You're right—you're all grown up now. Damn sexy, too."

Well, hell. Could he make it any worse? Struggling to form a response, she tried a joke. "Yeah, and I'm going to be one hot mama, too." She made a big, sweeping motion over her abdomen. "Just wait until you see me then."

He kept staring at her. Only now he was looking at her as if she was a specimen under a microscope—a pretty little organism he didn't quite understand.

"I've never touched a pregnant woman's stomach before," he said. "When the kid is kicking, will you let me feel it?"

The heat intensified, deep in her bones. "After your recent baby scare, I'd think you'd be more shy around pregnant women."

He shifted in his chair. "I'm just lucky they were already able to do a paternity test."

"Yes, you got lucky." Kara wasn't due for four more months, but there was no reason to wait for the baby to be born. They'd agreed on a NIPP, a non-invasive prenatal paternity test, where their blood had been collected to do a DNA profile on the fetus. They'd done it just nine weeks into her pregnancy. Tommy's brother, Brandon, had suggested the procedure. He was Tommy's attorney. Overall, everything had been kept quiet. Kara hadn't gone to the press, so Tommy had dodged that bullet, too.

He tugged a hand through his hair. "I'm just glad that poor kid didn't get stuck with me being its dad. Not just from an emotional standpoint, but with the way I travel, too. I'd feel awful if it was waiting around to see me, like Brandon and I used to do with our dad. I don't know how I'd cope with the distress it would cause. Some people take their kids on the road with them, but I couldn't fathom doing that, either."

"Me, neither." Sophie's mom had been prepared to stay home to raise her, but she'd died before she had a chance. "I want to be a traditional parent, tucking my son or daughter into his or her own bed every night."

"Yeah, I'm sure you'll do great. But at some point, your kid might wonder who its father is."

"I've already considered that." She'd spent every waking hour contemplating her options. "But I'm not sure if I want to use an open donor or not."

He sent her a blank look. "Open?"

"It's where the donor is open to contact with the child. But it can only occur after the child turns eighteen, and only if he or she requests to meet him."

"I wonder how much of a difference that would make. I guess it would depend on the type of guy the donor turned out to be. I think having no dad would be better than having a bad one. Or one who is barely around, or drunk or stoned, like my old man was most of the time."

"At least Kirby is trying to make amends and be a better father to all of you."

"He still has a long way to go, especially with Matt."

Sophie nodded. Matt Clark was the half brother in Texas whom Tommy and Brandon had never even met. Kirby had fathered Matt with one of his mistresses while he was still married to Tommy and Brandon's mother, which eventually resulted in their divorce. It was a long and sordid story that was going to be revealed in a biography Kirby had sanctioned about himself. In a strange twist, it was Matt's fiancée writing the book. She'd met and fallen in love with Matt while she was researching it.

Now that Tommy's tour had ended, they were supposed to have a family gathering at the Talbot compound sometime within the next few weeks to get acquainted with Matt. His fiancée was already there, working with Kirby on the book. Both Tommy and Brandon had met her a while back, when they'd agreed to be interviewed for the biography.

No one had asked Sophie to be part of the book. But she hoped that she could attend the upcoming gathering. She was curious about the son Kirby had kept hidden away from the world. At one point, he'd even abandoned Matt.

"So how does it work?" Tommy asked.

She blinked at him. "I'm sorry. What?"

"Choosing a donor."

She quit thinking about his family and focused on his question. "Sperm banks have websites with their donors' information. So all you have to do is search their catalog for donors who fit your criteria. In some cases, they'll provide childhood and adolescent photos of the donors. Some will even let you see adult photos. If the donors who fit your criteria are keeping their profile pictures private and you want your donor to resemble someone specific, you can send the sperm-bank photos showing what you want him to look like. Then they'll go through your donor choices and rank them by how closely they match."

"Really?" His lopsided smile resurfaced. "You should send in some pics of me."

"That's not funny." She swung her legs around and kicked his longue chair, rattling the base of it. She wasn't pleased that he'd put the idea in her head. She wouldn't mind if her child resembled him. He was beautiful to look at, with his straight, easy-to-style hair, greenish-brown eyes and ever-playful lips. There was also a gentle arch to his eyebrows, lending his features a comforting quality—when he wasn't making faces. She'd known him for so long that everything about him was familiar.

He leaned forward, resting his hands on his knees. He had an artist's hands, with long fingers. He played a mean guitar, but her favorite songs of his were ballads he'd mastered on the piano, with hauntingly romantic lyrics. He sang about being painfully in love, even if he didn't know the first thing about it. Sophie had never been in love, either, not where it tormented her soul or ripped her heart apart.

"Maybe I can help you choose a donor," he said.

She all but flinched. His suggestion caught her off guard, making her wonder what sort of nice-guy stunt he was trying to pull. "You want to help me select the father of my baby?"

"Sure. Why not?" He tilted his head nearly all the way to the side, as if he was sizing her up somehow. "Remember when I used to help you with your chemistry homework?"

"Yes, of course." He was good with numbers. Math and science came easily to him. "But this isn't a school project."

"I know." He righted the angle of his head. "But we're like family, you and me. The least I can do is support you on this however I can."

"Thank you." Suddenly she wanted to touch him, to put her hands where they didn't belong, to skim his exquisite jawline, to run her fingers through his still-damp hair. "That means a lot to me." More than it should. It even made her imagine him being the donor, which was about the dumbest thought she could've had. She wiped it out of her mind, but it spiraled back, undermining her common sense.

He asked, "Should we do it tonight?"

She struggled to comprehend what he meant. Her brain wasn't behaving. She was still stuck on the stupid notion of him being the donor, which was complete and utter lunacy.

"Should we do what?" she finally asked.

"Look through the sperm-bank sites. I'll ask Chef to make a batch of his double-chocolate-chip cookies, and I'll bring them with me. I know how chocolate helps center you."

"Yes, let's do it," she said, finally managing to rid her jumbled mind of the idea of having his child. "Let's go through the sites tonight." She needed to find a donor, a stranger.

And she was going to make sure it was someone who looked nothing like Tommy, someone who didn't have the slightest thing in common with him.

Two

Tommy sat next to Sophie at the computer desk in her home office, where they'd been for the past hour. She scrolled the donor search catalogs she'd bookmarked.

He could barely believe this was happening. Not just her wanting a baby, but the fact she was resigning as his tour manager. She was supposed to be a permanent fixture on the road, a constant he could count on. Sure, she would be an asset to his business management team. But that wasn't the same as her managing his tours. Life on the road was the soul of his existence, what he loved most about his job, and Sophie had always been part of it.

He studied her profile and the way her unruly hair framed her face, with one strand falling farther forward than the rest. He'd always been fascinated with her hair. When they were kids, she'd kept it short. She was just the cutest thing back then, following him everywhere he went. He wished that she was still trailing after him, instead of bailing out to have a baby.

So far, her donor search wasn't going well. She rejected one guy after the next. But Tommy didn't mind. He hoped that she might forget the whole idea, anyway.

With a sigh, she reached for one of the cookies he'd brought, dunked it in her milk and took a gooey bite. She kept dunking and eating until it was gone.

A second later, she licked the lingering mess from her lips, making him hungry to kiss her. Of course, that wasn't anything new. He'd been longing to taste that pouty mouth of hers since they were teenagers. If he thought he could haul her off to bed, he would strip her bare this very instant. Some people believed that sex between friends would complicate matters, but Tommy wasn't of that mind-set. Of course he had to consider Sophie's feelings, and he understood that being friends with benefits wasn't her style. She'd made that clear a long time ago.

He leaned closer to get a whiff of her perfume. She always smelled so sweet and good.

She shot him a wary frown. "What are you doing?"

He lied like a schoolboy. "You're blocking my view." Earlier she'd attached a large monitor, mouse and keyboard to her laptop to make their joint effort easier; he could see just fine.

"Sorry." She rolled aside her chair, obviously trying to make room for him. "Is that better?"

He nodded and made a show of looking at the screen, where her latest rejection, a surfer-type dude, offered his best smile. "Why are they all so young?"

"This particular bank only accepts donors in their mid-to-late twenties."

"And you're okay with that?" He didn't like the idea one bit. "It's as if you're robbing the cradle or something."

She shook her head. "What about you and those fine young groupies who worship at your feet? At least I'm only looking at these guys for—"

"How smart and handsome and virile they are," he interjected. As much as he hated to admit it, he was getting envious of the donors. It almost seemed as if she was searching for a lover. "Maybe you really should send in some pictures of me. You can dredge some up from when I was in my twenties." He paused for effect. "If you're lucky, there might be a match."

She sat back in her chair, giving him a disapproving look. "Gee, could you be any more conceited?"

"Don't act like you don't think I'm hot because I know you do." He grabbed the mouse and changed her search criteria, putting in physical features that matched his. He didn't care if he was annoying her. By now, she should be used to his pesky personality. "Let's see who pops up."

She turned away. "Do whatever you want, but I'm not interested."

"Yeah, right." He didn't believe that for a second. Sooner or later, she would sneak a curious peek.

He delved into his task. There were a variety of donors with his body type, as well as hair, skin and eye coloring. Not all of them had pictures available. He focused on the ones who did.

While he searched, Sophie wolfed down two more cookies. She was still avoiding looking at the screen. It didn't matter, anyway. He couldn't find anyone who fit the bill.

"Never mind," he said. "They're all dorks."

"Really?" She slanted him a sideways glance. "Every last one of them?"

He gestured to the monitor. "Take a gander for yourself."

"All right, I will." She settled back into place. "What about him?" She clicked on a candidate Tommy hadn't given a second thought to—a guy with longish hair and a one-sided grin.

He scrutinized the picture, wondering what the hell she was thinking. "He doesn't look like me."

"His smile does. His hair would, too, if he cut it and styled it like yours." She read the profile. "Oh, and get this? He performs in musical theater."

Tommy rolled his eyes. "Oh, right. That's all you need, for your baby to come out singing show tunes."

She laughed. "Now who's being a dork?"

"I'm serious, Soph. A son or daughter with his

genes could turn you into a stage mom. And if you think touring with me is tough, just think of how grueling your kid's Broadway ambitions are going to be. You need to steer clear of Mr. Musical Theater."

She called him out. "You sound jealous."

"Of that guy? My offspring would be way cooler than his."

She gaped at him. "*Your offspring?* I can't believe you just said that."

He hated that his chest had turned tight as he defended the remark. "I was just goofing around, trying to get your goat."

"Well, knock it off." Her voice quavered. Even her hands shook. "You're supposed to be helping me find a donor, but you're only making it harder."

He'd never seen her so worked up. This baby thing was messing with her emotions. With his, too, dammit. "So take Mr. Musical Theater and be done with it."

"I don't want him." She clicked away from the guy's profile. "I don't want anyone who has your smile. Or anything else that reminds me of you. I already…"

"You already what?" He prodded her to finish what she obviously didn't want to say.

She pushed her hair away from her face. "Nothing. I don't want to talk about it."

He wasn't about to let up. His stubborn streak was stronger than hers. "You better tell me. If you don't, I'm going to stay here day and night, bugging you for an answer."

"Why can't you just drop it?"

"Because I don't like seeing you this way." He wanted the old Sophie back, the woman who didn't freak out about everything.

She fell silent, and he waited for her to respond. Communication had never been a problem for them before.

Finally, she grimaced and said, "Earlier, when I was at your house, I had this crazy notion about you being the donor. It actually crossed my mind."

"Really?" He should have panicked, but somehow he didn't. If anything, he felt weirdly, wonderfully flattered.

She squinted at him. "Don't sit there looking so smug, not after telling me how cool your offspring would be."

"Sorry." He tried to seem less macho, even if he was still feeling his masculine oats. "I shouldn't have pushed it that far, but you were right about me being jealous. I don't like you searching for the perfect guy." He shrugged, still playing down his machismo. "I'm honored that you thought of me, though."

She got up and strode to the other side of the room. "It was the most insane idea I've ever had." She stopped and sent him a dubious look. "You're not thinking it could be possible between us, are you?"

"I don't know." His mind was whirring, the gears spinning inside his head.

She stood near a bookcase packed with Western

novels her dad used to read. Suddenly, she seemed so small and lost—a woman alone, missing her family.

"It'll be okay, Soph," he said.

She glanced up. "What will?"

"You finding the right donor and having the baby you want." Tommy considered the possibility of getting involved. Could he become her donor for real? Since he was on the road more than he was home, he would rarely see her or the child. That would make things easier for all of them, he supposed, with her being the sole parent. But he needed to be sure that the rules wouldn't change on down the line, that she would never ask more of him than he was capable of giving. "Let's say for the sake of argument that you did use me. Would it be a permanent agreement, with no expectations or daddy duties from me?"

"Yes, but you being the donor isn't going to happen. So why are we even talking about it?"

Flooded with feelings he couldn't deny, he went over to her. "Maybe it's supposed to be me. Maybe I'm the guy who's meant to do it."

She looked shocked. "You don't know what you're saying."

"Yes, I do." He knew exactly the direction he was taking, and somewhere deep inside, it felt right. "You've always been there when I needed you, working day and night, devoting yourself to my career. And as much as I'm going to miss you managing my tours and being on the road with me, it would be nice to know that I participated in making your baby dreams come true."

She looked as if she might cry. "That's really nice, Tommy, but you're making me feel vulnerable right now." She backed away from him. "And I have to keep my wits about me."

Had he already lost his? Offering himself up like that? His heart was beating triple time.

"Do you even know what being a donor entails?" she asked.

He gestured to the monitor, which had gone black. "I know as much as the guys on those websites do."

"But this is different. We're not strangers. In our case, there would be a lot more to consider, particularly with how entwined our lives are. I understand that you aren't interested in playing an active role as the father. I'm good with that, too. I want to be a solo mom. But would we tell the child who you are at some point? Or would you prefer to be completely anonymous, with no one ever knowing it was you?" She set her mouth in a grim line. "I couldn't make those types of decisions for you."

"And I can't make them on the spot." He understood there was a lot at stake, legal and emotional issues that could impact the future. He wasn't taking this lightly. "I need time to mull over the details, and once I've thought them through, we can discuss it further."

"It's just all so much." She seemed scared, uncertain if he could handle it.

He encouraged her to give him a chance. "Why don't we sleep on it tonight, and in the morning, we can both see how we feel?"

"Okay." She backed herself against the bookcase. "There's no harm in that, I guess."

He didn't move forward or invade her space. He kept a formal distance, even if he ached to press his body against hers. "I am sure of one thing. If I'm your donor, I don't want to use artificial insemination. I want to make that baby the natural way."

When her breath hitched, he knew that he'd just sent a surge of good old-fashioned lust through her blood. At least he had that in his favor.

"I don't know, Tommy. I just don't…"

He tried to help her relax by saying, "You don't have to decide now. I'm not trying to rush you. But I'm not going to pretend that I don't want to be with you, either."

"I'm more than aware that you've always wanted us to be lovers. And you know that I've always been attracted to you, too. But this is a lot to consider."

"Just think it over, and I'll see you tomorrow." Before she made an attempt to fall into step with him, he added, "There's no need to walk me out." He knew the way to her front door.

She nodded and let him go, without another word between them.

Sophie barely slept a wink. She'd spent most of the night wondering what to do. And now, at the crack of dawn, she stood in the kitchen sipping her second cup of coffee with unanswered questions still swirling in her mind. Should she refuse Tommy's offer and choose another donor? Would having a baby by him be too complicated or would it make the process easier? And then there was the sex. Should she give up the fight and sleep with him or keep it professional and insist on insemination?

So much uncertainty, she thought. So much she'd yet to figure out. But maybe all of her worrying and wondering would be for nothing. Maybe Tommy would revoke his offer, and the decision to use another donor would be made for her.

Preparing for that possible outcome, she retrieved her laptop and went into the dining room. Settling in for a brand-new search, she logged on to a different site from the one she and Tommy had used.

After sitting there for what seemed like forever, she glanced at the vintage cowgirl clock on the wall. Two hours had passed, and she hadn't found anyone who seemed right. Now that the donors were in direct competition with Tommy, she couldn't help comparing them to him.

Sophie heaved a sigh and reconsidered the musical-theater guy from the original site, but her attraction to him wasn't strong enough. She needed someone who could hold his own against Tommy, a man who made her heart skip a beat.

Which was stupid, she knew. Before Tommy had offered to be her donor, she wasn't concerned about being sexually attracted to the man she chose. But now that seemed to matter, somehow.

So maybe she should stop looking at donors with current profile pictures and focus on the ones who only had photos from childhood. Maybe that would solve her dilemma.

Unfortunately, it didn't. None of the kid pics looked enough like Tommy when he was young to make her want to choose the grown-up donor.

Dang it, she thought. Tommy had doomed her, ruining her chances of accepting anyone else. But there was still a lot to consider. If she used Tommy as her donor, they needed to discuss every aspect of what the future would entail. They'd already agreed he wouldn't play an active role as the father. But would he want to engage with the child in other ways? Or would he prefer to keep his identity hidden?

Whatever his decision, she was certain that they would always be friends. They'd know each other their entire lives. That was a bonus, particularly in a situation as sensitive as this one. Surely, between the two of them, they could make something like this work.

She could only hope that he hadn't changed his mind. She wanted him to be the donor.

Did that mean she was ready to sleep with him, too? God help her, she honestly didn't know.

Her phone pinged, signaling she had a text. She removed it from her shirt pocket. Tommy was up and wanted to come over now. She quickly replied to his message, as anxious as could be.

She considered changing her clothes, but decided to stay as she was, keeping it real. Her oversize men's shirt had belonged to her grandpa, and she wore it hanging loose over a pair of floral-printed leggings. Her shoes were fuzzy green slippers she'd bought at an offbeat boutique somewhere—she couldn't remember what city or state.

A short while later when the doorbell rang, she nearly skidded across the hardwood floor to answer it.

She flung open the door; the first thing she saw was both of her Pembroke Welsh corgis prancing on the porch. Typically, they came in and out through a doggy door in the den, but they were grinning at her as if they'd just rung the bell. Of course, it was Tommy who'd done it. He'd obviously let them into the front yard by way of a side gate.

The dogs scampered past her, but Tommy stood where he was, strikingly handsome in a simple straw Stetson. He towered over her five-foot frame. She always wished that she was taller, especially around him.

He shifted his booted feet. "How're you doing, Sophie?"

"I'm okay." She didn't want to admit that she was a basket case. "Doing the best I can."

"Me, too." His eyebrows rose slightly. "Are you going to let me in?"

She wasn't blocking the doorway, was she? She stepped back, realizing that she was. Struggling to get a grasp on her emotions, she led him to the living room.

He plopped onto the sofa, the leather upholstery creaking beneath his butt. "I hardly slept."

"Me, neither." She sat next to him, relieved that she wasn't the only one who'd tossed and turned. But she couldn't take any more small talk. "Are you still interested in being my donor?"

"I definitely am." As sunlight spilled in from the windows, his eyes changed color, turning from green to brown to green again. "What about you? Do you want it to be me?"

Sophie nodded. "Yes, I do."

"Good." He removed his hat and tossed it on the coffee table, making his eyes more visible. But at least they'd settled on a color. "There's a lot we have to discuss. Where do you want to start?" he asked.

With kissing you, her whirring mind answered. *With tasting the sexy slant of your lips.* Shaking away the traitorous thought, she said, "Let's start with the type of donor you decided to be."

He had a ready reply. "I want an open situation. No secrets, no lies. I don't want to mimic my dad, having a child no one knows about. I'd prefer that everyone was aware of our arrangement, including the kid when he or she is old enough to understand."

Sophie relaxed a little, feeling as if they were making headway. "I would've respected your wishes if you wanted to remain anonymous. But I agree that it would be better if everyone knew the truth."

"If you want, we can join forces to tell the kid. When the time is right, we can explain that even though I'm not in the traditional father role, I'll always be a family friend. With the way I travel, I won't be around that much. But at least he or she will know who I am and that I care about his or her emotional well-being. Plus, we can share our past, that you and I grew up together. I think the child would appreciate knowing our history." He smiled. "We can make this work. I know we can."

Her heart warmed. "Thank you, Tommy." She wanted to hug him for being so kind and conscientious. But she didn't trust herself to wrap her arms around him, not while the issue of how and when they'd conceive the child hadn't been resolved. She'd spent years keeping her desire for Tommy at bay, and she had to be careful.

He continued with his plan. "We're going to need a legal document to seal our deal. I can ask my brother to handle it. But if you'd prefer to seek your own counsel, I understand."

"I'm fine with Brandon representing both of us, if he's okay with it." He was like a brother, of sorts, to her, too. It was different with Tommy. There was absolutely nothing sisterly about her feelings for him.

Sophie frowned. Then why was she making such a fuss about sharing his bed?

Because he already had tons of women at his disposal, she warned herself, and she'd vowed to never be one of them.

Yes, but for the sake of conceiving her child, wouldn't it behoove her to make love with him?

As her pulse beat mercilessly at her throat, she rubbed the goose bumps peppering her arm. How many times had she fantasized about climbing onto Tommy's lap? Or sliding her hands down the front of his pants? Or making kittenish sounds in his ear? Sometimes she'd even thought about him when she was with other men, and she knew that was a terrible thing to do. Her last boyfriend had cheated on her, but in her low-down, dirty mind, she'd been unfaithful, too.

"Are you okay, Soph?"

She glanced up to find Tommy watching her. "I was just..."

He searched her gaze. "Making a decision about us?"

She nodded, struggling to keep her shameful appetite for him from running amok. "Maybe we should talk about—"

"Are you willing to sleep with me to make this happen? I don't want to pressure you. Maybe we should—"

"I'll sleep with you. But we're not having a random affair."

"I never said this was going to be random, Soph. We'll be doing this to make a baby. Granted, I've always wanted you, but I'm not going to lose sight of our agenda. I'd still like for it to be romantic, though."

She couldn't concentrate on how romantic he wanted it to be. She was trying to hold tight to her emotions. Even with as gentle as he seemed, he was still a playboy, and she was still the woman who was supposed to know better. Deflecting the romance, she said, "There will be certain times that'll be my best chance for conceiving."

"And when will that be?"

"In another week or so." Trying to alleviate the heat dashing through her veins, she presented the clinical side. "Most women ovulate in the middle of their cycle, with about five to six fertile days each month. When we're together, I'll use a test for accuracy."

He furrowed his brow. Clearly, she was talking over his head. "How long do you think it'll take?"

"For me to get pregnant? I don't know. But on the average, most fertile couples conceive within six months."

He tapped a finger against his mouth. "Maybe we should do it more often to be sure. When Mack and Jean were trying to have their kids, that's what they did."

"Mack told you that?" He was Tommy's drummer; she mostly knew him to be a private person.

"No. But at the last party at my house, I overheard Jean talking to some of the other band wives and girlfriends about it."

Sophie hadn't been included in that conversation. Of course, she wasn't one of the band wives or girlfriends, either. "You shouldn't have been eavesdropping on them."

"Are you kidding? I love to hear the stuff chicks yap about." He waggled his eyebrows. "So what do you say? Should we try Mack and Jean's method?"

The notion spun through her like a tornado. "Don't get smart, Tommy. Not now."

His expression became somber. "I know you're crossing a line you never intended to cross by being with me. And you're right—I shouldn't be cracking jokes. But I still think my idea warrants consideration."

"All right. I'll think about it. I might even discuss it with my doctor, to see what he thinks is advisable." She was trying to keep things in perspective, even if her body was hungry for his. "Also, there's one more thing. Before we go any further, you need to see your doctor and get a sperm-count test." She wasn't an expert on semen analysis, but she wanted to be sure there weren't going to be any problems in that regard. She'd already had her AMH level tested, making certain she was fertile. "The men on the donor sites are required to have above-average counts."

"Gee, nothing like putting me under pressure." He nudged her foot, tapping his boot against her slipper. "I'll do whatever you want me to do. Because one way or another, we're going to make a baby. And I promise we're going to have lots of fun trying."

She didn't doubt that. But for now, she needed to catch her breath. She stood and moved completely away from him, letting the gravity of the agreement they'd just made sink in.

After all of these years, they would finally be together.

Three

Eager to see Sophie again and share the results of his doctor's visit, Tommy drove to her house. Only three days had passed since they'd made a decision about the baby business, but if next week was going to be a prime time to conceive, he wanted to be ready.

He drove onto her ranch and parked, then hopped out of his truck and went into the barn. He'd texted her earlier, and she'd told him that was where she would be.

She was hard at work, mucking out a stall, and didn't seem to notice he'd arrived. He stepped back to admire her, with her dirt-smudged jeans and her hair coiled into a messy bun.

"Need some help?" he asked, announcing his

presence. He couldn't stand here all day like a teen-ager with his heart pounding.

She spun around. "Oh, my goodness, you scared me."

"Sorry. I didn't mean to sneak up on you."

"It's okay. I'm about done anyway." She finished the job and patted the mare in the stall.

After she put away the rake, she dusted her hands on her pants. Tommy always thought that she was a fine little cowgirl. When they were kids, she had the gumption to keep up with him, and that was saying a lot. He used to drag her along on his reckless escapades. And now, as adults, they were going to do the most reckless thing of all and make a baby.

She drank water from a canteen and asked, "So what's up? What important news do you have to tell me?"

"I saw my doctor, and my sperm count is great." Then in an old codger's voice, he jokingly added, "Those young whippersnappers on that donor site got nothing on me."

She rewarded him with a laugh. "Glad to hear it."

"So was I." He quit goofing around and glanced at a sensual line of sweat trailing from her neck and down into the opening of her blouse. The top two buttons were undone.

She gestured for them to go outside, as if she needed a change of scenery. He walked out beside her and waited a beat before he asked, "Did you call your doctor about what's advisable? About how often we should…"

"Yes, I called him." She hesitated before she added, "He recommends frequent encounters, especially during my ovulation window."

He moved closer and touched her cheek, marveling at how soft her skin was. "You're allowed to let down your guard and enjoy it, Sophie."

"I know." She met his gaze, and they stared at each other.

He lowered his hand. Suddenly he felt as overwhelmed as she looked. There was another subject he wanted to discuss with her.

They headed for a shade tree. The sun was already bright in the sky. She drank more of her water, and he braced his back against the trunk, feeling the rough bark through his shirt.

Finally he said, "There's something else I spoke to my doctor about."

"What is it?" She sounded concerned. "What's going on? Do you have a health issue?"

"No, it's nothing like that. But I've made a decision. After you have the baby and we know everything is all right, I'm going to get a vasectomy." He tried not to wince. The procedure itself gave him the willies, but the end result was important enough for him to follow through.

Her soulful brown eyes went big and wide. "Why would you do that?"

"Because I'm never going to be a donor again, and

I don't want to get caught up in another baby scare like I did with Kara, or accidentally make someone pregnant for real. I figured this way, there will only ever be one child in the world with my genes, and that kid will belong to you."

"I don't know what to say about that, Tommy."

"You don't need to say anything. I just wanted you to know that's what I've got planned. I also want you to know that I'm going to set up a trust for the baby, for when it's older."

She studied him in a way that made him feel emotionally exposed. Then she said, "That isn't necessary."

He shrugged, using humor as his shield. "With a donor as rich and ornery as me, the kid should get something out of it."

"You're not ornery." She spoke quietly, her voice as whispery as the breeze that had just kicked up.

"Maybe not, but I've got plenty of dough. And I want to make your son's or daughter's life easier."

"Thank you." She fussed with her hair, pressing some of the pins protruding from her messy bun back into place. "That's really nice of you."

He imagined her sprawled out on his bed and tangled up in his sheets, her long dark locks tumbling over a pillow. By now, the tiny trail of sweat between her breasts was making her cleavage glow. He looked away; he had to get control of himself. He knew he had to wait but she was making him hot and breathless.

"I'm going to Brandon's office this afternoon to

get his legal input." He'd already briefed his brother over the phone, but they were going to finish their discussion in person. "Do you want to go with me?"

"I can't. I'm meeting with Barbara today."

Right, he thought—to sort out the details of her new job. "Okay, then. We'll talk later, and I'll let you know what Brandon says." He had a pretty good idea of how her meeting was going to go. He'd already instructed Barbara to create a position for Sophie, giving her whatever she wanted. And Barbara, naturally, was delighted to do it.

She glanced toward her house. "I better go. I have to shower."

He merely nodded, and as she bade him goodbye, he envisioned her slick and sudsy and wet. He had to keep these fantasies about her in check until it was time. But on and off he'd been having them for years. In some form or another, Sophie was always on his mind.

Brandon's office was in the hub of Nashville, with a colorful view of the Country Music Hall of Fame and Museum.

The location served as a reminder of who they were, Tommy thought, and how this city impacted them. Their daddy was featured in one of the museum's galleries. Tommy was, too, with artifacts from his most successful tours. As for Brandon, he was an entertainment lawyer, representing the Talbots and other country heavy hitters. He was also an elected trustee at the museum. But Brandon had always been the high-class type, well-known and well-respected in Nashville society.

Tommy and Brandon had grown up in the same rich, privileged, crazy-ass house, but they were nothing alike. Still, they were as close as two completely opposite siblings could be. And lately, they'd banded together, helping their dad with his now three-year sobriety. They also supported their mom, a former supermodel, in her beauty-business endeavors, making investments and buying stock in her company. Mom had rebranded herself, and was starring in her own infomercials, selling cosmetics and skin-care products.

When Tommy first explained the donor situation over the phone, Brandon had reacted in a perfectly professional way. No personal opinions, no judgments. Even now, he was as cool as a corporate cucumber. He looked the part, too, in an impeccable gray suit, his short black hair slicked straight back, his chiseled jaw clean-shaven. He'd inherited regal qualities from their mother's side. Tommy didn't have any of that.

"I'd be glad to represent both you and Sophie," Brandon was saying. "I can draw up what's called a known-donor contract, clarifying the details you agreed upon. But first I'm going to consult with a colleague of mine who's versed in this area of law. I want to be sure there aren't any unforeseen events that we should include in the contract, things you and Sophie might've not considered."

"Whatever you need to do." He trusted his brother to get it done right. They were two years apart, with Brandon being older and obviously wiser. Besides, Tommy didn't like to fuss with the business end of things.

The wiser one squinted. "I hate to bring this up, but has Sophie thought about who she would name as the child's guardian in case she becomes incapacitated or dies? Family members are usually preferred, but Sophie doesn't have any family. And since you'll be signing away your rights, you wouldn't have any legal claim on the minor. Not unless you petitioned the courts, and with you not wanting to have a direct role as the father, I don't see you as doing that."

Tommy's gut tensed. The kid hadn't even been conceived yet, and now they were discussing the possibility of the child becoming an orphan. When he thought about how Sophie's mom had died, the tension inside him worsened. "I have no idea who she would name as guardian, but I'll bring it to her attention. Then she can consult with you about it."

Brandon looked him square in the eye. "Maybe she can appoint someone in our family. Mom would probably be willing to do it."

"Yeah, she probably would." Their mother was hoping for grandkids someday, and the likelihood was pretty damn close to nil if she had to rely on her sons. Brandon wasn't any more settled than Tommy in that regard. "Mom and Dad probably aren't going to like this donor decision of mine." He'd decided to wait to tell them until he and Sophie worked out the legal details, and now there was the guardian issue she would need to consider, too.

"No, I don't suspect they'll like the idea of you being a donor. Knowing Mom, she'll accept it easier than Dad will. She tends to be more pliable than he is. But it's your life, not theirs."

"Yeah, and considering the lives they've led, they don't have a whole lot of room to talk." Their parents used to have an agreement where their dad had been allowed to sleep with other women. Their mother's only stipulation was that he wouldn't father children with anyone except her, and he'd broken that vow when he'd sired Matt. "Do you think Mom was really okay with Dad screwing around like he did? Or do you think she just accepted it as part of what came with the territory?"

"I don't know. I've never asked her about it. But she'll be telling her side of the story in the biography, so it's all going to become public, anyway. From my understanding, Matt's mom has already been interviewed. Her story will be included, as well."

"Well, I think our mom is a darned fine person for forgiving Dad and choosing to be friends with him again. It's also nice of her to want to meet Matt and embrace him."

Brandon nodded. "It's going to be a heck of a get-together, all of us meeting up like that."

Tommy scrubbed his hand over his face. "Remember when Mom first told us that Dad had another son out there, and how we wondered about him?" They'd been teenagers at the time. Tommy had just turned sixteen and Brandon had been a diligent eighteen-year-old, the senior class president of the private academy he'd attended. Tommy had chosen to go to public school, where Sophie and the rest of his friends were. "I never hated Matt for existing, but I hated Dad for hurting Mom."

"I know how deeply it affected you. But everything about Dad has always been harder on you. You look more like him than I do. You're a performer like he is. You've had to fight your way out from under his shadow, even when we were young."

"It helps that I have a brother who understands." Tommy smiled. "And they say lawyers are heartless sharks."

Brandon flashed a lethal grin. "I have my moments."

No doubt he did. But all Tommy saw was the good in him. "You always supported me, even when I got into trouble."

His brother shrugged. "With the way you and Dad used to fight, I knew you needed someone on your side."

"Those fights aren't over yet. We had a raging argument not too long ago about Kara. He read me the riot act, even after I told him the baby wasn't mine."

"Did you call him on the carpet about Matt? About having a grown son he barely knows?"

Tommy blew out a sigh. "You bet I did. But he just babbled on about how much he's changed and how focused he is on being a dad now. For someone who's trying to atone for his mistakes and be a better parent, he doesn't have a clue how to go about it."

Brandon lifted a glass paperweight off his desk, looked at it and set it back down. "He's been sending me gifts. For all the birthdays and Christmases he missed back in the day." He glanced up. "Have you been getting presents from him, too?"

Tommy nodded. Along with a slew of other things, he'd received the same paperweight, containing a sentimental quote inside. "I know his heart is in the right place, but there's only so much of his interference I can stand. Even when I try not to argue with him, I still lose my temper."

"Do you want me to approach him about you and Sophie so this doesn't turn into a battle?"

As tempting as the offer was, Tommy declined. "I appreciate it, but you don't have to do my dirty work for me."

"Are you sure? I'm good at smoothing things over."

"Thanks, but I'll handle it." Tommy knew that he was doing the right thing by being Sophie's donor, and no one, not even his dad, was going to take that away from him.

* * *

Sophie cringed. Tommy and his father were snapping at each other, deep in the throes of a heated argument. Now she wished that she wouldn't have accompanied him to Kirby's house. Mostly she'd only gone with him so she could talk to his mother, Melinda, about being named as the guardian for her child.

But she hadn't gotten a chance to do that, not with the power struggle taking place between the men. Kirby didn't like their plan at all. He'd blown up the moment Tommy had told him.

Melinda seemed okay with the idea, or was at least being supportive, the way a parent should be. She'd tried to ease the tension earlier, but her efforts had been in vain. The whole thing was getting out of control, and Sophie didn't know what to do, either.

The four of them were in the main parlor of the plantation-style mansion, surrounded by the trappings of wealth and opulence. The entire compound had been dubbed Kirbyville by the press. Even the family had begun to call it that. And what a strange bunch they were, Sophie thought. There was nothing conventional about the Talbots, not with a patriarch like Kirby at the helm.

His maid had already brought in a pitcher of iced tea and served everyone, creating a formal atmosphere that had gone awry. Kirby looked like his usual legendary self, with his graying beard and signature black clothes. He paced back and forth, rugged and demanding. Melinda was dressed in white, making an angelic contrast to her ex-husband. At fifty-eight, she was as beautiful as ever, with her golden blond hair and tall, slim figure. She sat across from Sophie on a matching antique settee, heaving ragged sighs.

And Tommy...

He stood near a window, bathed in natural light, his hair mussed from running his hands through it.

"You don't know what the hell you're doing," his dad was saying to him. "It's not right."

"Oh, really?" Tommy countered. "This from the guy who had a secret kid with one of his mistresses?" He glanced at his mom for a second, as if to apologize for being so blunt in front of her. Then he glared at his dad again.

Kirby grabbed his tea and took a swig, as if he was gulping down the bourbon he used to drink. "I never planned on having a baby with Matt's mother."

"And that makes it okay? You lied to all of us, and later you abandoned him, as if he didn't matter. You're the last person who should be giving advice."

"Quite the contrary. I'm exactly the guy who needs to do it. I'm telling you, boy, if you're not going to be the child's father, then you need to remove yourself from the equation."

"Dammit, old man, I'm not a boy." Tommy set his jaw. "So don't treat me like one."

Sophie gazed at Melinda, and they exchanged uncomfortable glances. Nothing was getting solved.

Kirby polished off his tea, put the glass down with a thud and narrowed his gaze at his son. "After the last talk we had, I was hoping you'd start becoming more responsible."

"Responsible?" Tommy scoffed. "This isn't a case of me accidentally making Sophie pregnant, like you did with Matt's mom. We're entering into a legal agreement, with Sophie choosing to be a single mother. The baby will grow up knowing me as the donor and a close family friend, and if there's anything Sophie or her son or daughter needs, I'll provide it. I'm already planning on setting up a trust fund for the kid."

"And you think that's going to help?" his dad replied in a harsh tone. "I established a trust for Matt that didn't make a hill of beans. After he used it to get his ranch going, he paid back every dime, making damned sure I knew that he no longer needed or wanted my money. It's taken years for him to forgive me. So why would you purposely give up the rights to your son or daughter, possibly creating problems like that, too?"

"I'm giving Sophie the baby she wants," Tommy said, seething. "Why is that so hard for you to understand?"

"Because you're too close to the situation, and you're not thinking clearly."

Tommy stormed over to his dad, his dusty Western boots echoing on the pristine wood floor. He stopped just inches from his father and growled, "You don't know shit about what I'm thinking."

Kirby forged on, his voice getting louder. "I know that you're an adrenaline junkie who's always looking for a fix. And once you come down off this latest high, you're going to be left with a kid who isn't yours."

"It isn't supposed to be mine!" Tommy yelled. "That's the whole frigging point of me being the donor!"

Sophie wanted to tell both of them to shut up. She never used to argue with her dad, not even when she was a teenager. They'd always spoken kindly to each other. She would give anything to have him back. But it was different with Tommy and Kirby; they could fight about the weather. Granted, she understood that Kirby's views were distorted because of the mistakes he'd made with Matt, but his criticism wasn't helping. He needed to know when to quit. But Tommy needed to know when to cool off, too.

"Stop it!" Melinda finally made her way into the fight. She wagged her finger at her ex. "If this is what Tommy and Sophie want, they have every right to do it. They're consenting adults who can make up their own minds, and you need to stay out of it." She left her seat and sat next to Sophie. "I'm happy for you, honey. If you want a baby, then you should have one." She leaned forward to address her son. "And you'll make a darned fine donor."

"For crying out loud." Kirby threw up his hands. "You're all nuts."

For now, everyone ignored him. Tommy shrugged,

and then smiled at both Sophie and his mom. How quickly his mood changed once he got his way. But if it hadn't been for his mother, he would still be locking horns with his father. Trust a woman, Sophie thought, to save the day.

She still needed to talk to Melinda about the guardianship issue. Of course, she hoped and prayed that tragedy never struck, leaving her child in someone else's care. But she couldn't pretend that horrible things like that didn't happen, either.

Sophie turned to Melinda and said, "Brandon recommended that I appoint a guardian for the child in case anything ever happens to me. And since I don't have any family left, he suggested you."

"Oh, my." Melinda fluttered her hands in front of her face, her elegantly manicured nails glittering with silver polish. "Do you want it to be me, Sophie?"

"Yes, I do. I think you'd make a wonderful substitute parent." Sophie had friends with children, but they were so attached to their own families, she feared that if she chose one of them her baby would get lost in the shuffle. "My dad used to say how sweet it was of you, bringing me up to Tommy's nursery and sitting both of us on your lap."

"You were so cute together, always grinning at each other. You were just the prettiest baby. Tommy's nanny thought you were a doll, too, with those big brown eyes of yours." Melinda glanced at her son. "He always seemed happier when you were around."

She shifted her gaze to Sophie. "I'd be honored to be your child's guardian."

"Thank you." She blinked back tears. She hadn't expected this to be so emotional.

While the men remained quiet, Melinda softly said, "From what I knew of your mother, I really liked her. Kirby spent more time with her and your father than I did, with them being on the road together. In the beginning, I used to travel a lot, too, for modeling jobs, but I cut back after I had my kids. I didn't want to be an absentee mom."

"Me, neither. That's why I'll be working in the management office instead of going back out on tour with Tommy." She glanced at him, and he smiled. He seemed pleased that Sophie and his mom were creating a warm and gentle vibe.

Melinda turned to Kirby and said, "See, this is all going to work out fine."

He quickly replied, "Because Sophie asked you to look after her kid if she's not around to do it? I'm sorry to be so blunt, but that doesn't make everything all right. While she's alive and well, you're nothing to her baby and neither am I. We're not the grandparents, not if our son isn't the father."

Tommy jumped in. "Don't start, Dad."

Sophie spoke up, as well. "You're right, Kirby. You won't be the grandparents, not in a legal sense. But I'd be happy for both of you to get close to the baby. The way Tommy will be close, too."

"As family friends." Kirby plopped down next

to his ex-wife, crowding her and Sophie on the set-tee. "I guess it's better than nothing," he grumbled.

Melinda laughed a little. "I'm going to be the most doting family friend that baby will ever have."

"Me, too." Kirby chuckled. "An old, proud, grandpa-type friend." He shot Tommy a stubborn glance. "And nothing you can say is going to stop me."

"I'm not stopping anyone from doing anything. If Sophie says it's okay for you to spoil her kid, that's her prerogative." He came forward and sat beside her, making the settee even more crowded. He leaned over and whispered, "Thanks for indulging my parents."

"I don't mind," she whispered back. She was certain her family in heaven would approve.

As Tommy touched her hand, a sweet and sexy thrill shimmied through her. Now all she needed to do was conceive this much-anticipated child—with the baddest boy of country as her donor.

Four

Five days later, Sophie knew it was time. She appeared to be ovulating, based on the results of the test she'd just taken.

With her nerves ratcheted up a notch, she reached for her phone to call Tommy. As far as she knew, he was in his studio, toying around with some new songs. He never stayed idle for long. When he wasn't touring, he was writing or recording.

Sophie would be starting her new job next Monday, going into an office every day and working like a normal nine-to-fiver. Her life was on the verge of change, and if she was lucky, she would get pregnant right away.

Maybe even tonight.

She scrolled through her contacts and tapped

Tommy's name. With the phone on speaker, she listened to the line trill.

When they were in elementary school, he used to goad her into making prank calls with him. Back then, hardly anyone had mobile phones. Even caller ID was new. You could get away with all sorts of foolishness on those old landlines.

Tommy's phone went to voice mail, and she blew out a breath. With what they had going on, shouldn't he be more aware of the possibility of hearing from her and pick up?

Sophie didn't leave a message, mostly because she didn't want to say something so personal in a recording.

She sat on her bed, getting more anxious by the second. Her dogs kept running in and out of the room, chasing each other on their short little legs. With their smart and willful personalities, they could be quite bossy. But they were loyal to the core, too. Some people said that corgis weren't suitable for small children, but hers loved her friends' kids. She was certain they would adore her baby, too.

Pressure mounting, she debated calling Tommy again. But he beat her to it.

Her ringtone, an old Hank Williams Sr. tune, chimed with Tommy's name glaring across the screen.

Heart beating in her throat, she answered. A soft and floaty "hi" was all she could seem to manage.

"Hey, Soph. I got a missed call from you, and I—"

He stalled, as if her uncomfortable tone had just registered. "Is this it? Is this the day?"

"Yes." She wasn't being much of a conversationalist.

Neither was he, apparently. He went silent. An instant later, he asked, "When and where should we—"

"Tonight," she replied. "At your house." His master suite was a series of custom-built rooms; she'd been there plenty of times before. But this would be the first time she would get to explore his bed, his sheets, his pillows, his body.

That hot, hot body.

"Do you want to go out first?" he asked.

She cleared her mind. "I'm sorry. What?"

"You know, dinner and dancing."

Oh, my God. "Like a date?" She shook her head, even if he couldn't see her. "That isn't what this is about. Besides, you always get bombarded with people asking to do selfies with you. And I'd be too nervous to be in the thick of that."

"I was planning on taking you to a private club, where that wouldn't happen. But we can skip it if you're not up for it." He paused. "I don't want you to be nervous, Soph."

Too late. She already was. "I'm trying to relax."

"I can't wait to be with you tonight. To undress you." He spoke in a hushed tone. "It's all I've been thinking about."

"Me, too." But she couldn't sit here, tangled up in anticipatory knots, edging into phone sex with him.

The pulse between her legs was already throbbing. "I have to go, Tommy."

"Go where?"

Anywhere, she thought. "I have errands to run." That was a lie. The only place she needed to run was straight into his arms. "I'll see you later, okay?"

"What time should I expect you?" he asked, before she ended the call. "When is the bewitching hour?"

For a mysterious moment, she imagined creeping over there at midnight, casting dark-of-night spells. The moon was even supposed to be full.

"Sophie?" He was prodding her for an answer.

"How about nine? Or maybe eight would be better?" She couldn't decide.

"Eight," he confirmed. "I don't want to wait any longer than I have to. And you need to come hungry."

Her mind jumped. "What?"

"I'm going to feed you, nice and cozy, in my bedroom."

Was that a double entendre? "Are we talking real food?"

A smile sounded in his voice. "As real as it gets."

With him, one never really knew. "Dinner at your house?" She repeated it to be sure.

"In my bedroom," he reiterated. "I'll ask Chef to whip up something special."

So now he was arranging a different kind of date? She should have known he would have a backup plan. "You don't have to fuss over me."

"I'm doing it anyway. So just go with it, Soph."

Clearly, she didn't have a choice. He was taking control and sweeping her along, determined to start their baby-making affair with a romantic bang.

As evening rolled around, Sophie labored over deciding what to wear. She knew that her clothes shouldn't matter, not when she would only be removing them later. Still, she wanted to look pretty. Her underwear seemed especially important, so she rummaged through her drawer for her best lingerie—soft cottons with bits of ladylike lace. She didn't do the supersexy stuff.

After scenting her skin with a silky lotion and layering it with her airy perfume, she donned a cherry-red blouse and a short, chiffon-trimmed skirt, pairing the ensemble with Western boots.

She plaited her hair into a long, loose side braid, with unbound tendrils falling around it. For makeup, she went for a sheer bronzer, a light coat of mascara, a hint of blush and lipstick that complemented her blouse.

Sophie gazed at herself in the mirror. Was it too much? Should she undo her hair and change into something less frilly? In spite of Tommy's interest in wining and dining her, this wasn't a real date, and she wasn't supposed to be getting romantically invested in it.

She looked at her reflection again. Her outfit was nice, bright and pretty. So she needed to stop worrying about it. With the effort she'd taken to get ready, she should just stay as she was.

Earlier, Tommy had sent a text telling her to use the private entrance to his house, the one that led directly to his suite, from an outdoor stairway near the pool.

Sophie packed an overnight bag, but that didn't mean she was staying the night. She might skip out after the sex and return to her own safe little haven. It depended on her mood and if she needed to escape.

She drove to Tommy's place, taking the same route she always took. But it felt different. Bumpier, she thought. Not the road, but her emotions.

When she arrived at the main gate, security buzzed her in.

She made her way to the back of the mansion and took the designated staircase, stopping on the landing to glance out at the pool and the brightly lit waterfalls. From her vantage point, the entire grounds looked spectacular, with their flourishing greenery, vibrant southern gardens and long and winding riding trails.

Instead of knocking, she tried the knob on the door that would take her into Tommy's suite and found it unlocked. She was familiar with the layout and knew how expansive it was. She entered a marble-floored sitting room with silvery gray sofas and shiny black tables. The hallway beyond it offered a media room, a library and a music room, each designed for Tommy's personal use. Somewhere in the middle was a glass elevator. Then, finally, at the end of the hallway, she would encounter his bedroom—complete with a fancy dining alcove, a luxurious bathroom built for two, separate dressing rooms for him and his lovers, and a breathtaking balcony.

She didn't mind that he hadn't come out to greet her. It made her feel independent to go to him. Then again, for all she knew, he was watching her on a security camera in his room and getting a thrill out of it. She'd heard rumors that he had voyeuristic tendencies, but she'd never been brave enough to ask him if they were true.

Sophie actually had fantasies about being watched, but she'd never told him that. She'd never admitted it to anyone. She was way too shy to act out her fantasies, unlike Tommy, who probably did all sorts of wild stuff.

She ventured down the hall, feeling like a virgin on a warped wedding night. But thank goodness that wasn't the case. He wasn't her first lover, and they were nowhere near being married. She was only having this mini affair with him so she could get pregnant. She almost laughed to herself. As if that scenario was so much saner.

Almost there, she thought, as she stopped in front of the big, beautifully carved double doors to his room.

She rotated the brass handle on the right one and crossed the threshold. There was no turning back now. She was in for the count, or the date, or whatever the heck this was.

Sophie gasped. The room was dimly lit with burning candles, in different shapes and sizes and colors, scattered everywhere. She made her way to the dining area. The table was elegantly set, and a portable food-warming cart stood nearby, the entrées covered with metal lids. Another cart presented a small but fully stocked salad bar. The third unit offered a decadent assortment of desserts. There was a beverage-and-coffee bar, too, with a refrigerator and stainless-steel sink built into a wall.

She looked around for Tommy, but didn't see him. She didn't see his chef or a maid or anyone else, either.

Maybe Tommy was on the balcony. Or maybe he was taking a last-minute shower and getting dressed. She took a moment to check out the main course, lifting the lids on the entrées. It was three of her favorite Italian dishes: chicken marsala, gnocchi with red sauce and baked artichokes stuffed with Parmesan-seasoned bread crumbs.

"Evening, Sophie." Tommy's voice sounded behind her.

She closed the lid on the artichokes and spun around. Suddenly she realized that he'd been there the entire time, sitting in a darkened corner of the room. She could see him now, gently illuminated in a pale gold light he'd just turned on.

"You're cheating," she said. "Catching me off guard like that."

"I just wanted to enjoy the feeling of watching you." He stood and left his wingback chair.

He definitely seemed like a voyeur. But instead of viewing her on a security camera, he'd waited until she entered his room, observing her in person. Sophie got desperately aroused. But the feeling was wrapped in a dangerous sensation, too, with how easily it triggered her fantasies.

He looked incredibly handsome, dressed in a classic white shirt, a Western bolo tie and black trousers. But as sharply attired as he was, he hadn't gotten ready all the way. His feet were bare. Call her crazy, but that struck her as sexy. It was just so...*Tommy*.

"Everything looks wonderful," she said. Him, his room, the food.

"So do you." He came closer. "So beautiful." He leaned in and whispered, "I can't wait to make love with you."

She nearly teetered in her boots. "You're supposed to feed me first."

He nuzzled her cheek. "Are you hungry?"

"You told me to come hungry." His whiskers scratched her cheeks. But she better get used to it. He always shaved with one of those trendy trimmers, creating perfectly even stubble. She knew a lot about his personal habits. Too much, she thought.

He turned his face more fully toward hers. Was he going to kiss her? Or was he being playful, letting her soak up the heat between them? She was already tingling.

"What are you doing?" she asked.

"I want to kiss you," he replied.

"Then do it," she said, a millisecond before his lips crushed hers.

Sophie moaned beneath his onslaught. Quick and wet and wild, he pillaged her mouth. He tugged her tight against him, and she kissed him back, her tongue sparring with his.

This had been years in the making. The buildup, the desperate desire had always been there, below the surface. And for now, it was only a kiss.

While her mind spun, Tommy toyed with her braid, pulling it gently, then roughly, then lightly again, keeping his mouth fused to hers the entire time.

So good, she thought, so hot and dizzying.

But it didn't last. He broke the connection and let her go. She blinked at him, struggling to breathe.

"Now we can eat," he said.

Sophie blinked again. He only smiled and turned away.

"Do you want wine?" He headed over to the wet bar. "I brought up a bottle of merlot for you."

"Yes, please." She could definitely use a drink.

He uncorked the bottle and poured the rich, red liquid. He handed her the glass, and she took a much-needed sip.

"Have a seat, and I'll serve you."

"Thank you."

He fixed her salad and brought it to her. He tossed

his, too, and filled their water glasses from a chilled pitcher, garnished with lemons.

"Did you know that there are hundreds of fertility gods and goddesses from cultures all over the world?" he asked. "I got curious and looked some of them up."

She couldn't help being intrigued. She settled her napkin on her lap. "Do you have a favorite? Someone we should call upon tonight?"

"Venus would probably be pleased to hear from us. She's the most widely known. Aphrodite, too. They're similar in nature, but are from different origins. Roman versus Greek. Also, from my understanding, Aphrodite is more of a sexuality goddess than one of fertility." He scooted in his chair. "I like her for sure."

"Yes, I'll just bet you do." She dug into her salad, fascinated.

"Overall, I think Liber is my favorite. He presides over male fertility. There was even a cult that worshipped phalluses in his honor. His female counterpart is Libera. They're Roman deities who represent liberation and being wild and free." He gestured to her merlot. "They're gods of wine, too."

"Then I'll enjoy this in their honor." She toasted him with her glass. "You should write a song about them."

His voice turned low, rough and carnal. "I think I'd rather write one about having this affair with you."

Sophie didn't reply, but somewhere deep down, she wanted to be the subject of one of his rebellious songs.

They finished their salads in silence. He served the main courses, and she studied him from beneath her lashes. He was watching her, too.

Once it was time for dessert, she said, "Maybe we should share the pastries. In bed," she added softly. She needed to get closer to him, to do away with the table between them.

He took an audible breath. "Whatever you want, Soph." He got up and approached the pastry cart.

She left her chair and walked over to him. "Let's try a few bites of each." She wanted to tempt her palate in as many ways as possible.

He arranged a mini fruit tart, a chocolate éclair and a slice of marshmallow pie on a glass plate. He studied his masterpiece, before squeezing in a caramel-pecan cannoli. "Now, that's a sugar overload."

"It's perfect." She followed him to his massive four-poster bed. All of the furniture in his room was big and heavy and ornately carved.

He placed their desserts, two gold forks and two linen napkins on a nightstand. "I think we should unmake the bed for later." He lowered the quilt and fluffed two pillows that already looked gloriously soft. "We should get more comfortable, too." He unfastened his bolo tie and took it off. He untucked his shirt and opened the buttons, leaving the tails hanging loose.

Sophie joined in, pulling off her socks and boots.

"That's it?" he challenged her. "That's all you're getting rid of?"

"We're not playing strip poker. But if you insist on treating it that way, then how about this?" As brazen as could be, she reached under her skirt. Then, without letting him see anything, she peeled off her panties. She flung them a distance away. "Game over."

He gaped at her, and she smiled. It felt good to tease him. But she still wanted her sweets. Perched on the edge of the bed, she took a creamy bite of the pie. She was going to taste the éclair and the tart next, saving the cannoli for last. But for now, the pie was delish. She fluffed up another forkful. "Want some?"

"No." He plopped down beside her. "You've got about two seconds to finish that before I pounce."

She held the untouched bite between them. "We're supposed to be sharing dessert."

"It's too late for that." His voice vibrated with anticipation. "You can't sit there, so nice and polite, after whipping off your panties like that, and not expect me to go mad."

Sophie should have known better than to bait him. With a man like Tommy, she was bound to lose. But she was enjoying the game, too.

"Hurry up and eat it," he said.

With a burst of excitement, she shoved the marshmallow filling into her mouth, swallowing it quickly. She'd never been so aroused.

He grabbed the fork away from her and speared the éclair with it, causing the custard to seep out.

Then when the fork toppled over, it jarred the plate and sent the cannoli rolling onto the floor.

Ignoring the mess he'd made, he nudged her down, slid his hand under her skirt and kissed her deep, causing her pulse to skyrocket.

He used his fingers, making her wet, teasing her with his foreplay. He didn't stop, not until he flipped up her skirt in one fell swoop.

"Do you want more, Soph?"

"Yes." *Please, yes.* Her modesty was all but gone. She was fully exposed to his view.

He went after her blouse. "Let's finish getting you naked first." Her bra came next. Then her skirt. He blew air over her stomach as he pulled it off. "Now I can ravage you for real." He lifted her legs onto his shoulders and pulled her against his mouth.

She tunneled her hands through his hair, the intensity of his touch rippling through her. He used his tongue like a warm, slick weapon. he licked; he swirled; he stabbed; he kissed.

Sweet heaven, he was good at this.

A waxy scent from the candles filled the room. She inhaled the aroma, flames dancing to and fro.

He glanced up at her, making the connection stronger. She kept her eyes open, wanting to see him, too. Steeped in sensation, she leaned forward, putting her fingers near his mouth. She wanted to touch the source of all that wicked pleasure.

So much warmth, so much wetness.

Sophie couldn't have stopped the orgasm if she tried. She came in a series of long, gasping shudders.

Tommy waited until the last wave subsided before he sat up.

"Do you know how long I've wanted to do that to you?" He spoke softly, sexily.

She was too hazy to respond. Her mind had gone numb. She could barely move, barely think.

He undid the button on his trousers, and her brain kicked back into gear. She took a thrill-seeking peek at the bulge pressing against his zipper.

"This is going to be a first for me," he said.

She adjusted her line of sight, zeroing in on his handsome, sharply defined face. "A first what?" she asked, her voice coming out raspy.

"I've never been with anyone without protection." He removed his shirt and tossed it onto the floor. "But tonight I'll be skin-to-skin with you."

A newly awakened pulse fluttered between her legs. "I've never done it that way, either." She'd always insisted that her lovers use condoms. Not just for birth control, but to stay safe in other ways, too. "Do you think we'll notice a difference?"

"I don't know. But we're about to find out." He ditched his pants, peeling off his crisp white briefs with them.

He was big and hard, beautifully endowed and already beading at the tip. She reached down to stroke him. When she spread the moisture in gentle little circles, she felt him shiver.

He touched her, as well, roaming his hands along her curves. He climbed on top of her, fondling her breasts and licking her nipples. She opened her legs, making more room for him, and he lifted his head.

They looked into each other's eyes. By now, he was poised at the juncture of her thighs.

"My Sophie," he said.

Her heart pounded. "I'm not supposed to belong to you."

"It's just for tonight. And every other day or night that we're together." He skimmed his mouth over hers, whispering against her lips. "Then it'll be over."

She wrapped her arms around him, and he entered her. But he didn't move. He just stayed there, letting both of them savor the moment.

"It does feel different," she said. There was an unsheathed closeness she couldn't deny   warmth of the most intimate degree.

"Oh, yeah." He pushed deeper. "Oh, hell, yeah." He angled his hips for their mutual pleasure. "I'm going to try to make this last, but it still might happen fast."

She met his gaze. He already had a feral gleam in his eye, his hair falling rebelliously over his forehead.

"But you're going to come lots of times tonight," he continued, nipping her earlobe.

"Promise?" She was more than ready, eager and willing.

"Definitely." He rocked her body with his, setting a passionate rhythm.

Holding him to his promise, Sophie dug her nails deeper, eager to take every mind-spinning, heart-hammering, love-making thrust he gave her.

Five

The reality of being with Sophie went beyond Tommy's expectations. He couldn't get enough. He wanted more and more of her, of this feeling. Every nerve ending in his body had come alive, sparking beneath his skin. She matched him stroke for stroke, lifting her hips and taking him deeper.

In his mind's eye she was part feline, a beautiful hellcat, using his back as a scratching post. Even her hair—that pretty braid and the messy strands falling around it—drove him crazy.

She moaned, and he rolled over the bed, taking her with him and tangling the sheets. He changed positions, so she was on top. He wanted her to ride him as wildly as he'd been riding her. It was her turn to buck and spin.

She didn't miss a beat. She straddled his lap, moving up and down, giving him a cowboy's thrill. He watched her, captivated by the fullness of her breasts, the flatness of her stomach and roundness of her hips. Tommy gripped her waist, and she bit her lip in naughty concentration. Then he reared up, putting his face next to hers. They kissed on contact. The exchange was sloppy, but deeply carnal, too. He slipped his hand between their bodies and rubbed her where it counted.

The kiss ended with a jolt of electricity, and she latched on to his shoulders. Was she anchoring herself for the orgasm that was building inside her?

"I can't… This is…" She struggled to speak.

She couldn't what? Stay grounded while she came? He rubbed her a little softer, a little sweeter, giving her a moment to breathe. She slowed down the pace, riding him in a more languid way. Like silk over skin, he thought.

Sophie came softly, her lashes fluttering, her body shimmying. Tommy skimmed her cheek, so damn glad she was his friend. He couldn't imagine a world where she wasn't in it.

When the final wave subsided, she put her head on his shoulder. He eased her down, switching positions again. She looked up at him, and he reentered her.

A new dance. A new awakening.

No matter how fast or slow or easy or frantic their rhythm was, it worked. She wrapped her legs around his waist, and he pumped into her. They were compatible as lovers, even though this could never last beyond their attempts to conceive.

They kissed and caressed and made hungry sounds. By now, he knew every lovely inch of her, mapping her for pleasure. He made her come another time, pleased with how responsive she was. But finally, Tommy needed a release, too.

So damn badly.

On the heels of Sophie's most recent orgasm, his muscles went taut, as his mind was consumed with lust. He inhaled the scent of sex, her heat mingling with his. He caught a misty veil of her lingering perfume, too.

So light, so pretty.

As his vision fogged, he gazed at Sophie, trying to keep her in his sights. She seemed to be watching him, too, in the same blurred way he watched her.

Tommy came, feeling strong and invigorated, knowing his seed was spilling deep and warm inside her.

After he was spent, he kissed her, then fell into her arms. She stroked a hand down his back, soothing the scratches she'd put there.

A few beats later, he rolled off her. But he remained close, right beside her, where he intended to stay for the rest of the night.

He trailed a hand along the flare of her hip and asked, "Do you want to finish dessert now?"

"Thanks, but I'm good." She stretched, as agile

as the hellcat she'd become in his mind. "I should probably leave soon, anyway."

He frowned at her. "What are you talking about?"

She sat up and held the sheet against her. "I left my bag in the car, in case I decided not to spend the night."

"And now you decided to go home? Come on, Soph. Don't leave."

"But I don't want to get too cozy, to make too much of this."

He tried to persuade her to stay once again. "There's nothing wrong with a little coziness. Afterglow is supposed to be this way, isn't it?"

"Yes. But this isn't a real relationship, and we already did what I came here to do."

"That doesn't mean you have to dash off in the dark."

"I guess it wouldn't hurt to stay." Her expression softened. "I'm just a little nervous, cuddling with you like this. It's all so new."

"There's nothing to fret about. We both know the rules, and a little cuddling isn't going to change anything."

"Then I'll have to go to the car and get my things."

Because he didn't trust her to skip out on him, he said, "I'll get it in a while. And don't worry if there's anything you forgot to pack. I've got plenty of toiletries you can use. I'm well stocked with guest supplies."

"Right. The big bad musician and all of his overnight guests." She shook her head. "I shudder to think of how many women have slept in this very same bed with you."

"You knew who and what I was when you agreed to be with me."

She made a face. "Boy, did I ever. But I only agreed because of the baby."

"Yeah, and I'm still the best guy for the job." He tried to ease the tension by tugging on her braid.

She poked a finger into his ribs. "There you go, being conceited."

"About me being the right guy for the job? That's just a fact. And you know what else? I should make you eat the rest of the pie you teased me with. You and your seduction trick with the panties." He feigned offense. "It was shameful."

"Really? Well, I should make you eat the éclair you took a stab at with your fork. Look at that poor thing."

He glanced over at the nightstand. The éclair was a bit of a disaster. The pie looked sort of pathetic, too. The cannoli was definitely a lost cause, smooshed up on the floor. "The tart hasn't been touched. Maybe I'll eat that instead."

"You can't wolf it down without giving me some."

"I thought you didn't want any more dessert."

"That was before you convinced me to stay the night." She practically pushed him out of bed. "Go get it and bring it over here."

"One romp in the hay, and I almost forgot how bossy you can be." Amused, he leaned over to kiss her.

She returned the favor, and they tasted each other with their tongues. A minute later, he grabbed the tart, along with both forks. They sat cross-legged on the bed, bare-ass naked, sharing the treat.

Tommy smiled and stole a strawberry from Sophie's side of the tart. She nudged him away, and he laughed, immersed in the long-awaited exhilaration of this moment.

Sophie was glad that she hadn't gone home. It was still strange, though, to be snuggled in Tommy's bed. But at least she didn't feel the urge to escape. Odd as it was, she was enjoying their postsex rapport.

"Do you think we made it happen?" he asked, gesturing to her stomach with his chin.

"Your guess is as good as mine. But it can take some time."

"A guy can hope." He lifted one shoulder in a brawny shrug. "Will you feel anything right away if it does happen?"

"I have no idea." She smiled and ate more of the tart. "This is yummy."

"I wonder what food cravings you'll get. My mom said she used to crave Mississippi mud pie when she was pregnant with me. But I think she made that up because I was always covered in mud when I was a kid."

She remembered being covered in it with him, especially after a good hard rain. "Actually, mud pie is a great craving. I could do worse."

"Wouldn't it be funny if you craved me?"

She glanced up from her fork. "What?"

"I was just saying that it'd be funny if you craved me instead of some sort of food. But I'll be off-limits by then, so you better have me out of your system before you're waddling around with my donor bun in the oven."

"Your donor bun?" She laughed. Sometimes he had the goofiest way with words.

He laughed, too. "You know what I meant."

Yes, she did, indeed. And she agreed about getting him out of her system. When this was over, she needed to be done with him. No more sex. No more cozy afterglows.

They finished the tart, and he set aside the tin. After that, he propped a pillow and leaned against it.

Struck by his nonchalant pose, she said, "Just so you're aware, pregnancy doesn't make women crave men. So you better get that thought out of your head."

He shrugged. "You might be the exception."

Lord, she hoped not. She didn't want to crave him after she was pregnant. It was bad enough wanting him now. In the silence that followed, her mind spiraled in a new direction, one she hadn't expected to take. And just like that, she asked, "What's Kara like?"

Tommy merely stared at her. "What?"

Sophie couldn't blame him for his reaction. She

had sprung the question on him; she wasn't even sure why she'd asked it. "I was just wondering what kind of person she is. With all this pregnancy talk, it made me think of her, I guess."

He sighed. "Truthfully, I hardly know anything about her, except she's a bartender at the Miami hotel where we hooked up. It was such a quick thing, we didn't spend a lot of time chatting each other up. But I can tell you this much—I don't think she wanted her baby to be mine. I called her after the DNA results came in, just to see how she was doing, and she sounded relieved that I'd been eliminated as the possible father."

She contemplated Kara's plight. "Maybe she cares about the man who turned out to be the real father. That could be the reason she didn't go to the press."

"I don't know. Maybe. I didn't ask her about him. I didn't think it was my place. But calling her still seemed like the right thing to do." He ran a hand through his hair. "Should I get your bag now?"

The quick change of topic threw her, but she understood how it was a sensitive subject for him. "Sure. My keys are in my purse." She stood up to get them while he climbed into a pair of sweat shorts he removed from a drawer.

"You can blow out the candles while I'm gone," he said.

"Okay." They certainly couldn't leave them burning all night. "They were a nice touch, Tommy."

He smiled and came over to kiss her. She melted

from the sensation, from the taste of his lips, then warned herself to stop being so girlie. But darn it, being close to him felt good. For now, she told herself it didn't matter. As soon as she conceived, their intimacy would end.

He left the room, and she extinguished the candles. Keeping busy, she picked up their clothes from the floor and placed them on a chair. Without thinking, she put on his shirt and rolled up the sleeves. She buttoned it, too, keeping the fabric next to her bare skin. She was being girlie again. But she didn't want to remove it.

When Tommy returned, Sophie was clearing the table and stacking the dishes in a rack on the bottom of the salad cart.

He set her bag near the bed and dropped her keys back into her purse. "Look at you," he said, roaming his gaze over her.

Yes, look at her, traipsing around in his shirt. "I was just borrowing this for a second." She fingered the hem. "But I can put my robe on now. It's in my bag."

He approached her. "You can stay like that. It looks better on you than it does on me. And you don't have to fuss with the dishes. I was going to do that."

"It's all right. When I'm finished, you can wheel the carts into the hallway and call the kitchen to have someone pick them up." She knew that was Tommy's habit when he dined in his suite. It was similar to being in a five-star hotel.

After everything was done and the room was clear, Sophie said, "I'm going to remove my makeup and get ready for bed."

"I have to do that, too. Not the makeup part. But I need to brush my teeth and whatnot."

They went into the bathroom together. Since it had been designed for Tommy and his lovers, there was lots of elegant space for separate routines.

He finished before she did, but he didn't return to the bedroom. He sat on the edge of the freestanding tub and observed her every move, making her self-conscious. But she liked it, too. The forbidden feeling of him watching her.

She went ahead and said, "I heard rumors that you were a voyeur or something."

"Not the way you're suggesting. I'm not a Peeping Tom or anything." He smiled his crooked smile. "Get it? *Tom? Tommy?*"

Of course she got it. She reached for her moisturizer and asked, "Then what do the rumors mean, exactly?"

He moved his gaze up and down her body. "I just think it's sexy when my lovers...you know..."

Touch themselves and let him watch? Sophie clutched the bottle in her hand, holding it tighter than necessary. What he'd just implied was her deepest, darkest fantasy. The manner in which she often imagined being watched.

Should she tell him? Should she admit it? No, she

thought. She would rather keep it a secret, especially since she wasn't brave enough to actually do it.

She looked in the mirror and saw that her skin was flushed. Of all things, she was blushing. Her nipples were hard beneath her shirt, too. Or Tommy's shirt, as it were. But thankfully, it was baggy enough to conceal what was happening. She didn't want him to know how this was making her feel.

She hurried up and finished her routine. She didn't even take her hair out of its braid. It was easier to just get the heck out of the bathroom.

Once they were back in his bedroom, he asked, "Did you make a wish when you blew out the candles?"

She rummaged through her bag and found the short, simple nightgown she'd brought. "Isn't that only for birthday cakes?"

"I don't know, but why are you putting on clothes? Don't you sleep naked?" He was already peeling off his sweat shorts.

"Typically, no." And this wasn't the time to start.

"Then why don't you just sleep in my shirt instead? You can unbutton it to make it more comfy."

So that she would be seminaked?

He walked over to her. "I'll do it for you."

She stood like a statue while he made the adjustment. Heaven help her, but she could scarcely breathe. Her fantasy was rattling around in her head all over again. But she needed to stop thinking about it.

"That's better." He dusted his fingers over her

protruding nipples. They were showing through the fabric now. "Are you cold?"

"A little," she lied. She was still aroused by him.

"I can warm you up." He led her to bed, and they got under the covers. He spooned with her, pressing the front of his body to the back of hers. "How's this?"

"It's nice." *So very nice.* She was tempted to turn around and initiate another round of sex, but she closed her eyes instead. There was something incredibly sweet about being held by him.

Sweet and complicated, she thought. For such a rough and reckless man, Tommy had a dreamy side. He reached across her to turn out the light and then settled back into place, where they slept for the rest of the night.

Sophie awakened in a breathless flutter. Tommy had one hand wrapped around her breasts and the other resting low on her stomach. She barely had time to open her eyes, to focus on the light creeping into the room, let alone assess the situation.

Was he awake and aware of what he was doing? Or was he asleep? In case it was the latter, she kept still, trying not to disturb him. But either way, she liked the position she was in. Her pajama top, the shirt she wore of his, was riding up in the back, and his morning erection was pressed against her bottom.

She had no idea what time it was, but it seemed early. It hadn't taken much for him to talk her into sleeping there. She'd given in easily. But that had always been the nature of their relationship. Tommy could convince her to do just about anything.

As the hand on her stomach moved, sliding toward the V between her legs, Sophie took a stirring breath. He must be awake. Surely he didn't play around like that in his sleep. Then again, with Tommy anything was possible.

When he started peppering her neck with suckling little vampire kisses, her pulse jumped. He knew exactly what he was doing.

"Oh, my," she said, her voice coming out crackled. "That feels good."

"Uh-huh." His response sounded rough, too. By now, he was spreading her with his fingers, getting ready to stake his masculine claim.

Sophie knew that she shouldn't be reacting to him with such desperate passion. He had more than enough women who flocked around him. But she was here for the sake of her baby. It was different for her.

Different or not, he was making her eager for more. Of course, Tommy had lots of practice. She even remembered the first time he'd gotten laid and how jealous she was. Not that he'd had sex, but that he'd done it with the prettiest and most popular girl at their school.

She closed her eyes, struggling with the memory. She could have been with him back then, too. She'd just been smart enough to refuse his advances.

He took his hand away, and she opened her eyes. Had he sensed what she'd been thinking? God help her, but she didn't want him to stop.

"Tommy?" she asked in a concerned tone.

"It's okay, Soph." He whispered against her ear. "I just want you to get on your hands and knees so we can do this right."

Without hesitation, she removed the shirt so it didn't get in their way and climbed on all fours. He got behind her and steadied her hips as he rubbed against her. She arched her body, anxious to feel him inside. But first, he undid her braid, removing what was left of the plaiting and letting her hair cascade over her shoulders and down her back. Then, on something akin to a growl, he pushed all the way inside.

Sophie keened out a moan. She'd been taken this way before, but it hadn't been as primal as this. With each and every thrust, he tugged on her unbound hair.

She pushed back against him, meeting his determined strokes. He was at the right angle to stimulate her G-spot. But sex god that he was, he probably already knew that.

Soon he was doing all kinds of wild things—reaching around to fondle her breasts, biting her neck, scraping his teeth along her collarbone.

Sophie was on the verge of losing her mind.

She came hard and fast, jutting and jerking against

him. Primed and ready, Tommy exploded, too, groaning and growling and spilling into her.

In the moments that followed, she collapsed head-first onto the bed. He scooped her into his arms, and they both rolled over, face-to-face once again.

Sophie relaxed in the bath, or she tried to. The tub was certainly big enough to accommodate two people, so that wasn't the problem. It was Tommy. They were seated across from each other, and he kept staring at her.

She splashed some water at him. "Knock it off."

"Knock what off?" He tossed the soap in her direction, and it landed directly in front of her.

"Looking at me in that hot-and-bothered way of yours." She tried to grab the floating item, but he leaned forward and retrieved it.

He sat back and said, "I have no idea what you mean."

"Yes, you do." He couldn't play the innocent. She knew him far too well. "We just had sex, and you're still thinking dirty thoughts."

"So I'm a guy with an active mind." He placed the French milled soap back in its dish and braced his arms on either side of the tub. The way he reclined made him look regal, like the Nashville prince that he was.

Gorgeous and oh-so idolized.

She sighed. "Maybe we should talk about something else."

"All right." He ran a damp hand through his hair. "We can discuss our schedules and plan for what's ahead. I think you should move in with me while we're trying to conceive."

She blinked at him. "You want me to stay with you?"

"Not forever. I'm just trying to make the baby-making process easier. It might help for it to happen spontaneously instead of us having to arrange it every time."

He probably had a point. But for now she couldn't think clearly.

He continued, "You can bring the dogs and horses, the way you always do when we're on tour. This is already like a second home to them." He drew up his knees. "Think about it, Soph. We're going to be together as much as we can, and it doesn't make sense for us to bed-hop when we could be in the same house."

And his mansion was the logical choice, of course, with how big and private and secure it was. "I don't know. It just seems so…" She didn't know what word she was searching for. All she knew was that she'd never imagined living with him, not even temporarily. But there was a part of her that liked the idea. It seemed oddly thrilling, somehow, to always be ready for each other. And if it helped make the baby…

"Did you tell Dottie about us?" she asked, wondering what to expect if she stayed here.

He shook his head. "I didn't tell Chef Bryan, either. They didn't know who I was entertaining last night. But since we're not keeping our arrangement a secret, I was planning on mentioning it to them today. Come on—move in with me. And as soon as you're pregnant, you can go back home."

"What if it takes six months to conceive?"

"What difference does that make? We've practically lived together before. Growing up together as kids, and then all those years on the road."

"None of that is the same as our current situation." Of going to bed together each night. Of waking up beside each other every morning. "You've never even had a girlfriend who's lived with you."

"I know. But that's the beauty of it. We're not a couple. We're just making a baby. And we're used to each other, Soph. I mean, really, how bad can it be?"

As bored as he got when he wasn't on tour? It could get bad, she thought. But maybe she was worrying for nothing. He was right about how much time they'd spent together in the past. That definitely counted for something. "All right, we'll try it. But only for the first month, as a trial period, just to see how it goes."

He smiled. "That works for me."

"I just hope we don't get on each other's nerves." Or that she didn't start enjoying it more than he did. With his restless nature, there was no way to be sure.

"I think it'll be fine." He swirled his hand in the bath. "The water is cooling off. Should we have Chef send up some breakfast, then go back to bed?"

She laughed a little. "You're insatiable."

"I can't help it if I'm hungry." He swooped across the tub to kiss her, sloshing the cooling water.

When his mouth sought hers, she latched on to his shoulders, pulling him closer.

She was hungry, too.

Six

Sophie had been living with Tommy for nearly a week. So far, they'd made love every day. At some point they would take a break and rejuvenate, but for now he wanted to make the most of their time together.

He glanced over at her. They were both getting dressed, putting on casual clothes. Today they were going to Kirbyville to meet Matt. Tommy had invited Sophie to join him for the family gathering, a picnic by the stream his dad had arranged.

He was feeling overwhelmed. Not just about meeting Matt, but about how things were playing out with Sophie. Was she enjoying his company? Was their arrangement working for her?

"Am I getting on your nerves?" he asked.

"What?" She sent him a baffled stare.

"You said before that you hoped we weren't going to get on each other's nerves, so I'm just checking to see where your head is at now."

"I only said that because of how restless you get when you're not on the road. By next week, you're probably going to be bored out of your gourd."

"Are you kidding? Sex with you is never going to bore me."

She batted her lashes. "My own personal sperm donor."

He laughed. "Darned right." He strode over to her, reached out and put his hand on her stomach. "I wonder if it happened yet."

"It's too early to tell." She looked into his eyes. "And to answer your question, you're not getting on my nerves. I like playing house with you."

"Is that what we're doing?" He splayed his fingers, where her baby would grow. "Well, whatever it is, I'm glad you're coming to the picnic with me."

"So am I. I want to meet Matt and his fiancée. Her name is Libby, isn't it?"

He nodded. "She seems nice enough. She has a six-year-old son. He's supposed to be there, too."

"I didn't know she had a child."

"I guess I forgot to mention the boy to you." Tommy was still trying to grasp the details himself. "Dad told me that Libby is widowed. That she lost her husband about three years ago."

"Oh, how sad. What's her son's name?"

"Chance. And get this—his middle name is Mitchell."

"Chance Mitchell?" Sophie's eyes went wide. "Like the fictitious outlaw from your dad's song?"

"Yep. Libby and her late husband were fans of my father's. She's probably going to be the only one at the picnic who hasn't been hurt by my old man."

She sat on the edge of the bed to put her boots on. "Kirby has never hurt me."

Uncertain about her remark, Tommy asked, "You aren't hurt that he doesn't approve of our donor arrangement?"

"I'm disappointed that he thinks we're making a mistake. But I'm not hurt."

He grabbed his boots and sat next to her. "I totally forgot to tell you that Dad called this morning. He wanted to know if he could include us in the biography."

"Us? As in you being my donor?"

He nodded. "He made a valid point about the time line. The book is scheduled to be released next summer, and if everything goes as planned, you'll be pregnant or maybe even ready to give birth, and we would've made a public statement by then."

"Do you think that's what we should do?"

"Contact the media ourselves? Definitely. I'd rather take things into our own hands than let the press put a spin on it. I can have my publicist handle it when we think the time is right. But for now, I'll have everyone who is aware of the situation sign a nondisclosure so it doesn't get leaked before we're ready to share the information." Tommy knew how easily people could turn on you and sell your story for personal gain. He knew how brutal the gossip sites could be, too. "If we agree to have it included in the book, Kirby said that we can tell our side of it. But he wants to be able to state his opinion, too."

"And tell the world that he wishes that the child was going to be his official grandbaby? I suppose we can't fault him for that." She sighed. "Has he already confided in Libby about it?"

"Yes, but it won't go into the book unless we say it's okay. But I don't think it'll matter, either way. The biggest part of the biography will be the unveiling of Dad's secret son, not the baby you'll be having."

"Well, thank goodness for that." She tossed him a smile.

"Yeah. You know Dad. He wouldn't dare let us upstage him in his own book." As cute as her smile was, he couldn't help but frown. "So are you ready for this little family gathering?"

She reached for his hand and squeezed it. "I think the real question is if you're ready."

He avoided the issue. Instead, he said, "Dad already took precautions to keep the picnic private and away from the press, so no one needs to worry about that. He doesn't think anyone would suspect who Matt really is, anyway. As far as Dad's household staff knows, he's just Libby's fiancé who comes to visit her when she's there."

"That's not what I meant about you being ready for it. I was talking about you meeting Matt."

He finally admitted how he felt. "Honestly? I'm nervous about making a favorable impression on him. I'm not like Brandon. He always gets people to warm up to him. I don't know how to do that, not without pouring on the celebrity charm, and Matt isn't going to give a crap about that."

"Just be yourself, Tommy."

"But that is who I am." A superstar's rebellious kid who'd blasted his way to the top, too. "You've seen me in action all these years. You know that I'm not good at being a regular guy. If I'm not performing or being the life of the party, I don't know how to act around people."

She kept holding his hand. "If it's any consolation, Matt is probably as nervous as you are."

"No doubt he is." But Tommy was still worried that he was going to be Matt's least favorite brother.

By midafternoon, the picnic tables were laden with leftover food and the family had divided into separate groups. Sophie and Tommy's mom were engaged in girl talk with Libby, and Brandon, Matt and their dad were goofing around with six-year-old Chance and playing tag in the grass. Tommy was the odd man out, just as he'd suspected he would be. He'd barely exchanged more than a few words with

Matt. He didn't know how to interact with Chance, either. He'd never been particularly good with kids. So instead of joining the men, he walked beside the stream, letting the breeze skim past his face.

What the hell was wrong with him that he couldn't just behave like a normal guy? Even his dad was pulling it off. Not that Kirby was in any way average. He used to do weird things, like wear his sunglasses in the house. Not all the time, but often enough for Tommy to recognize the signs of his old man's hangovers. Dad used to find all sorts of ways to shut out the family. But today, Kirby looked like Grandpa of the Year, with how easily he was playing with Libby's son.

When Matt took a break from tag to grab himself a cold drink, Tommy decided to approach him. Matt was only going to be in Nashville for a few days, and he would be spending most of that time with Kirby. If Tommy wanted to make a halfway-decent first impression on his brother, he needed to do it today.

He headed over to Matt, and as they stood beside the cooler, Tommy asked, "Will you grab me a bottle of sparkling berry water?"

"Sure." The Texan reached into the ice chest and handed him one.

"Thanks." Tommy twisted the cap, and they gazed awkwardly at each other. Matt was tall, like Tommy, with a long, lean frame, but other than that, they didn't resemble each other. The other man had short black hair, dark skin from his mother's Cherokee side and stunning amber-colored eyes. He owned a recreational ranch in the Texas Hill Country that was a major success, but he still carried himself like a down-home guy.

"So how's it going?" Tommy asked. It was all he could think to say.

"Fine. How's it going with you?"

"I'm all right." But this conversation was stilted. They both took a swig from their drinks.

After a beat of silence Matt said, "Everyone says you're like him."

Tommy hated the comparison to his father. "I'm not. Or maybe I just hope I'm not. He can be such an SOB at times, with that arrogant manner of his."

Matt smiled for a split second. "Yeah, I know." The smile didn't return, not even a flicker. "He treated me awful when I was a kid."

"He wasn't a good father to me or Brandon, either. I used to fight with him, where we'd get right in each other's faces. We still do that, even now."

Matt glanced over his shoulder. "Brandon seems to get along with him okay."

Tommy followed his line of sight. Kirby and Brandon were swinging Chance by his hands and feet and making the kid laugh. "Brandon makes more of an effort than I do. He's the peacekeeper."

Matt turned back around. "And what are you?"

"The daredevil, I guess. That's what I'm known for, even within the family. Brandon and I used to refer to you as our lone-wolf brother. We always wondered what you were like."

"To be honest, I always wanted brothers or sisters, but not strangers who only shared half of my blood." Matt shifted his stance. "It was hard for me to think of you as anything other than Kirby's legitimate sons. But now I know that you were just as miserable as I was being his kid."

Tommy barked out a humorless laugh. "I'm still miserable about it." He quietly added, "If I was you, I never would've forgiven him."

"I had to work at it, believe me." Matt blew out a breath. "Mostly I did it for Libby and Chance. I knew that I couldn't be a strong and loving husband to Libby or a kind and caring father to Chance if I was harboring hatred toward my own dad. I had to make things right. It was important to Libby, too. She's gotten to know a side of Kirby that no one else has, with how deeply he's confiding in her for the book. She knows he's screwed up, but she sees how much he cares and how sorry he is."

"Sometimes I see it, too. And other times, he just seems like a pompous ass, poking his nose into my life."

Matt nodded. "When I first reunited with him and told him that Libby and I were getting married, he took credit for our relationship. He actually patted himself on the back about it. He brags about Chance being named after his song, too. But he is wonderful with the boy. Chance thinks he's cool."

"I can tell." Tommy noticed how the kid hung all over Kirby. "He's not taking credit for anything I'm doing right now. He's pissed at me for what I've got going with Sophie. I know that he told Libby. Did he tell you about it, too?"

"The sperm-donor arrangement?" Matt furrowed his brow. "Yeah, he mentioned it. But I think you have a right to do whatever you want to do."

"Being a donor suits me." He glanced back at Kirby, who was still playing happily with Matt's new stepson. "I don't want to end up like Kirby, having children I don't know how to raise. It's better if Sophie parents the child on her own."

"I always wanted kids. I was even married once before to a woman who had two little twin girls. But it didn't work out. She divorced me within six months. She wasn't who I was meant to be with."

"I'm not meant to be with anyone. Sophie and I are just friends." Friends and temporary lovers, he thought. And for now, he was content to have her as his housemate, too. He shook his head. "I can't believe I'm having a personal discussion like this with you."

Matt made a tight face. "As much as I hate to say this, I used to think of you as an idiot. I never liked your public persona."

Tommy laughed in spite of himself. "Sometimes I don't like it, either."

Matt laughed, too. "I'll keep that in mind." His expression sobered. "It's going to be tough when the book is released and everyone finds out that I'm Kirby's son. Dad said that we can do some press conferences ahead of time and announce it beforehand, but it's still going to disrupt my life. As much as I hated being his secret kid, I got accustomed to it."

"I guess we're all accustomed to the roles he has us playing in his life."

"I used to ban his music at the barn dances at my ranch. I never let the band cover his tunes. Your music was off-limits, too. But I'm letting that rule go now."

Curious, Tommy asked, "What reason did you give for banning our songs?"

"I never said, but I think people drew their own conclusions, assuming that the Talbots' music reminded me of something bad from my past. They just didn't know how bad it really was. I didn't even tell my ex that I was Kirby's kid or that you were my brother. Only Libby knows."

"I'm sorry that you felt that way." Tommy didn't want his music to be a source of anyone's pain. "But I'd love to see your ranch someday."

"That'd be great. You're welcome anytime. But if you visit sooner rather than later, we'll have to stick to a cover story about how we know each other. We can't admit that we're brothers until after my identity is revealed."

"We can just say that we became acquainted through Libby since she's my dad's biographer and you're her fiancé. We can tell everyone that we're newfound friends." Tommy paused to add a silly joke. "Unless I'm too much of an idiot for that."

Matt flashed a teasing smile. "You're not so bad."

"Ha. You say that now. You only just met me." But at least they were off to a good start, taking steps toward the future, where they could actually become real-life friends.

After the picnic ended, Tommy and Sophie returned to his house. She followed him into his music room, where he tuned one of his prized guitars, and she scanned a music trade magazine from the 1950s. Tommy had a huge collection of them. But he could tell from the way she was absently paging through it, she wouldn't stay quiet for long. Tommy was in a reflective mood and was being silent. He got like that sometimes, especially after emotional encounters, and today had been chock-full of emotion.

As expected, she set aside the publication and said, "I had a nice time. It seemed like you did, too, after you got over that hump with Matt."

Without looking up at her, he adjusted the Stratocaster on his lap. It was a prototype of the signature model that had been designed for him, with plans to market them next year. "It turned out better than I expected. But I made a conscious effort to talk to him."

"Yes, I noticed that you sought him out."

He finally lifted his gaze. "You were keeping tabs on me?"

"Not the entire time, but I wanted to be sure you

were doing okay. I've gotten used to having you on my radar."

It wouldn't be like that once he started touring again. He wouldn't be anywhere near her radar. He didn't want to keep dwelling on that, though, not with as much as he was going to miss traveling with her. But at least he was helping her to have a baby. Whenever he was on the road, he could envision her with her child, being happy as a single mom. "What did you think of Libby?" he asked, taking his mind in another direction.

"I adored her. I mean, really, what's not to like? She's upbeat and smart, with a glittery sense of style, white-blond hair, big blue eyes and two perfect little dimples. I can see why Matt fell head over heels. Then again, he's quite the catch, too."

Tommy felt a pang of jealousy. "So he impressed you, did he?"

"Oh, my word, yes. Not only is he tall, dark and broodingly handsome, he's thoroughly devoted to Libby and her son." Sophie leaned back in her overstuffed chair. "He's everything they need."

Tommy got up and placed the guitar back in its case. When he returned to his seat, he said, "I guess you're going to look for a guy like that someday?"

"Are you serious? I'd never find anyone who wants me that badly. Besides, I just need to focus on being the best single mom I can be."

"A lot of men would want you, but I'm glad you've got your priorities straight." He couldn't stand the idea of a stranger coming along and sweeping Sophie off her feet.

"Libby wasn't looking for anyone, either. But still, her situation was different from mine. She didn't set out to be a single parent." She sent him a coy smile. "And for now, I'm just happy I have you as my baby-making lover."

"Oh, right." He scoffed, even if her remark warmed him in all the right places. "Now you're kissing up to me? After you swooned over my brother?"

She rolled her eyes. "I wasn't swooning. I just think it's nice that Matt and Libby found each other. Mostly what she talked about was how amazing Matt is with Chance. Isn't he just the cutest thing? A ball of energy, but so bright and clever, too."

"He seemed like a sharp kid. But children have always been a mystery to me."

"He reminded me of you when you were that age—not as mischievous, but there was just something about him."

"What I remember most about being six is us being in first grade together. I was afraid that we might not be in the same class, but we were." For all the good it had done. He'd yapped so much to her, their teacher had separated them, putting him on the opposite sides of the room. "You never got in trouble, but I was always getting a time-out."

She laughed. "I wasn't the one disrupting the class, Tommy. You were."

He shrugged, trying to brush it off. "I can still be disruptive, I guess."

"You guess?" She wagged a finger at him. "You make everyone crazy with worry. Every time you step out on stage, it's another broken bone waiting to happen."

"I've never gotten that busted up." Just a few typical injuries, he thought, and certainly nothing that had stopped him from performing.

"It still makes me crazy."

"Then we're even because you make me crazy, too." If he'd gotten her out of his system years ago, he probably wouldn't be so damn attached to her now. "Sexy crazy," he clarified.

She stared at him for a second. "I knew what you meant."

Before things got awkward, he said, "I guess it's safe to assume that Matt and Libby are going to have more kids. That Chance will have brothers or sisters."

"Oh, most definitely. Libby told me that they're going to get married first, though, and the wedding isn't scheduled until next year. They want time to plan it right." Sophie paused for a second, then prattled on. "Libby is originally from California, so she and Chance relocated to Texas to be with Matt. But since she's been spending so much time here with Kirby on the book, Matt has been looking after Chance when she's gone. He's really close to her son."

"So I gathered." This was the second time Sophie had mentioned Matt's tight-knit relationship with the boy.

She tucked her feet under her, getting cozier in her chair. "When Matt and Libby get married, Chance will be your nephew. Kirby already treats him like a grandson."

"I noticed that, too. But I'm not surprised, not with how my old man is champing at the bit to be a grandpa." He squinted at her, thinking how pretty she looked, with her now-wrinkled picnic attire and long hair in a ponytail. "It's funny how people can be crappy parents, and then end up being wonderful grandparents."

"Some folks mellow with age. And in your dad's case, I'm sure it has a lot to do with his sobriety."

Tommy nodded. He'd hated having a drunk and stoned father more than he'd ever hated anything. "I just hope he never starts drinking or using again."

"He seems really committed to staying clean and sober."

"For now, he definitely does." But lots of alcoholics and addicts fell off the wagon. "I think that's why my mom is able to be friends with him again."

"It was great that she was at the gathering today. She really liked Matt and Libby. And she thought Chance was a doll, too." A moment later, she asked, "Did you know that Matt competed in junior rodeos when he was a kid?"

"No. We didn't talk about anything like that."

"You ride and rope, too."

"But I never competed." He wouldn't have been able to follow the rules. "I'm not a structured-sports guy. Never was, never will be."

"I know, but Matt is teaching Chance to ride and rope, and I was thinking that maybe someday you could teach my son or daughter to be a cowboy or a cowgirl, too."

The gravity of this conversation was making him nervous. What if her child didn't give two figs about him? It wasn't as if he was going to be the dad. "You can do that, Soph. You ride and rope as well as I do."

"Yes, but what I learned, I learned from you. So that's why I thought you could teach my child, too. That seems like something a family friend could do, and since that's going to be your role in his or her life…"

"Sure, okay. But only if that's what the kid wants." Tommy was already concerned about overstepping his bounds. There weren't any hard-and-fast rules for family friends, not like there were for dads.

She glanced around the room, settling her gaze on the piano, before returning her attention to him. "Maybe you can teach the baby to play music, too."

He battled a quick, shaky breath. He hoped her son or daughter didn't blame him for not knowing how to be a parent. "The way I tried to get you to master 'Chopsticks'?"

She primly folded her hands on her lap. "At least I tried."

He chuckled in spite of how he was feeling. "Who

are you trying to fool? You were the most impatient student I ever had."

"I was the *only* student you ever had," she countered.

That was true. He didn't share his skills with just anyone. "Let's hope that kid of yours inherits musical aptitude from me."

"I hope it inherits a lot of things from you."

"You do?"

"Of course," she softly replied. A heartbeat later, she winced. "But if it's a boy, it better not be a womanizer. That's a quality I don't want my son to have."

Instead of taking offense, Tommy combed his lusty gaze over her. "I should seduce you for even saying that."

She turned flirtatious, too, making naughty eyes back at him. "Here, in your music room, amid the instruments I don't know how to play?"

"Hell, yes." He stood and dragged her out of her chair, backing her toward the piano. "We're going to make our own wild brand of music."

She laughed, and they kissed, hard and rough. After they yanked off each other's clothes, he pressed her bare butt against the piano keys and said, "If you're not pregnant already, you sure as fire will be."

Just as soon as they were done.

Seven

Sophie wanted to cry. On this quiet October morning while she was getting ready for work, her period came.

Determined to stray strong, she pulled herself together and took the elevator to the first floor of the mansion, where a buffet-style breakfast was being served. Tommy had already gone downstairs ahead of her. In fact, he'd gotten up early to ride a new mare he'd bought, so she hadn't seen him since he'd rolled out of bed. He'd taken her dogs with him, letting them run around in the yard today.

As she reached the dining hall, she spotted Dottie coming toward her. The older woman smiled and said, "Tommy is back from his ride and is having his breakfast in the garden room. He'd like you to join him there."

"I will. Thanks." When the urge to cry returned, she bit back the tears. She had no business getting upset after only a month of trying. But still, she felt cheated. She wanted so badly to be pregnant.

"Are you okay?" Dottie asked. "You seem sort of sad."

"I'm fine. I just have something on my mind." She couldn't reveal what was wrong, not without telling Tommy first. "I'm going to grab my food now."

"All right, hon. Chef made a lovely spread today with the sweet-potato-and-spinach strata you like so well. He enjoys having you here, and so do I. Just let us know if there's anything else we can do for you."

"Thank you. That's sweet. You've both been so accommodating." She wanted to put her head on Dot's shoulder, but that would provoke the tears she refused to cry. "I'll talk to you later. Okay?"

"Sure." Dottie walked away, returning to her household duties.

Sophie fixed herself a plate, taking an extra helping of the dish Chef Bryan had prepared specially for her. She also went for crab cakes and avocado sauce. She added fresh fruit and whole wheat toast, along with a frosty glass of milk. She'd already had coffee in Tommy's suite.

She put everything on a tray and carried it to the garden room, located just off the dining hall.

Tommy sat at a mosaic-tiled table, surrounded by

a spectacular array of plants and flowers, with several fountains bubbling nearby. He looked exceptionally rugged wearing his Western riding gear in this glamorous setting.

He glanced up and noticed her. "Hey, there."

"Hi." She put her tray on the table and took the chair across from him. When she unfolded her napkin on her lap, she skimmed her stomach and frowned. Instead of dragging out her news, she hurriedly said, "I just got my period." To keep those stupid tears at bay, she sipped her milk.

"Damn. Really? I was so sure that we were going to…" He moved around a half-eaten crab cake on his plate. "It'll happen next time."

"What if it takes longer than we anticipated? What if it goes on for years or never happens at all?" Nature was difficult to predict, and now a fearful burst of gloom and doom was setting in.

"Come on, Soph," he admonished. "Don't talk like that."

"But what if that's our fate?" Or more accurately, *her fate*. He wasn't the one who wanted a baby. "You're not going to keep doing this with me forever."

"I'll do it as long as it takes. I already told you that."

"Yes, but years? Come on, Tommy. It's unrealistic for you to think you could stand it for that long."

"Stand what? Having you as my lover? Or console you when you get your period?"

Both, she thought. But she said, "Maybe I should just go back to my own house."

He scowled. "You're giving up already?"

"No, but it might be less emotional if I wasn't living with you."

He stared across the table at her, the fountains gurgling in the background. "Don't you like being here?"

Truthfully? She loved the pampered warmth he provided, and that was beginning to seem like a problem, too. What if she started getting crazy ideas about living here for real? She wasn't supposed to be a permanent fixture in his home. "I just don't want to overstay my welcome." Or get more attached to him than she already was.

"You're not overstaying anything. I want you here, Sophie. I want to see this through, the way we originally planned."

She debated what to do. Maybe once her period ended, she would be able to think clearly. Besides, how much more attached to Tommy could she get? They'd been ingrained in each other's lives since they were born. "All right," she conceded. "We'll keep things as they are for now. But I can sleep in one of your guest rooms until we start working on the baby again. We don't have to keep sharing your bed."

He shook his head. "Don't be ridiculous. You're sleeping beside me, just like you've been doing." He resumed eating. "So now that we got that over with, I have something to ask you. There's a fund-raiser I'm supposed to attend later this month. You know how I hate those stuffy high-society balls, but Brandon gave me the tickets. It's an art auction, and I promised him that I would buy something. He can't attend because he has another event that night. Anyway, I thought it might be more interesting if you joined me." He paused. "So, will you be my date?"

"Do you think that's wise? Us dating like that? People might misunderstand and think that we're a bona fide couple."

"What people? Everyone close to us knows we entered into a donor agreement and that you're living here for now. The assumption is that we're sleeping together, anyway. That's part of why I had everyone sign nondisclosures. Even the management team you work with signed them."

That was true. He'd taken the necessary steps to stop people from talking about them. "What about the press? If there are any photographers there, our pictures might show up on gossip sites."

"Don't worry. That's not going to happen."

Did that mean this was a carefully screened event? It certainly seemed so. She relaxed a bit. "Okay, I'll go with you." Maybe it would be good for her to have an evening on the town, to get dolled up and get out of the mansion, to quit stressing about their relationship seeming real. They would be back to the baby-making business by then, too, and that was her priority.

"Great." He tossed her a boyish grin. "Since the media won't get wind of it, we can dance really close and kiss and make sexy spectacles out of ourselves."

She shook her head. Even if they weren't in danger of ending up on gossip sites, she wasn't going to get wild at a charity ball. "We're going to behave, Tommy. No PDAs."

He didn't reply. He drank his orange juice and gazed at her over the rim of the glass, as if he was daring her to do it when the time came.

Sophie felt like Cinderella getting ready for her famous ball. Tommy had brought a beauty expert to the house to do her hair and makeup. He'd purchased a designer gown for her. He'd also made certain that loaner jewels were available. She'd gotten dressed up for award shows and industry parties and whatnot in the past, but not where Tommy had hired a stylist for her or orchestrated what she would be wearing. No matter how much she tried to squelch the Cinderella feeling, it wasn't something she could seem to shake. Of course, it wasn't as if Tommy was her fairy godmother. She even laughed at the thought.

Her appearance wasn't anything to snicker at. This was the most elegant she'd ever looked. She stood alone in the private dressing room designed for Tommy's lovers, gazing into a full-length mirror. Her hair was swept into an intricate updo, and her champagne-colored, mermaid-style gown was embellished with hundreds of shimmering glass beads. She'd chosen a red garnet bracelet and diamond drop earrings as her accessories. Her heels were red, with shiny gold soles.

Suddenly, she caught a tall, dark reflection behind her. *Tommy.* He'd just entered the dressing room.

He stayed quiet, admiring her from where he stood. Attired in a classic black tuxedo, he held a delicate red-rose corsage.

Her handsome date bearing a gift.

She turned to face him, and they gazed silently at each other. He moved forward to put the flower on her wrist.

"Thank you," she said. "It's beautiful."

"You're the one who's beautiful." He lingered over her. "I have something else for you."

He led her out of the dressing room and over to the bed. On top of it was a champagne-colored mask that matched her gown.

She stepped forward without touching the mask. It had long, red fluffy plumes incorporated into the design. "We're going to a masquerade ball? Why didn't you tell me before now?"

"I wanted to surprise you."

"Now it makes sense why you said us being seen together won't matter. If we're wearing masks, no one will know who we are."

"Yes, but don't get too excited. It's still going to be the same stuffy function." He picked up the mask and handed it to her. She held it against her face, and he tied it into place.

"How does it look?" she asked.

He circled around to face her. "Gorgeous. Sexy." He opened an armoire equipped with a mirror. "See for yourself."

She turned and saw a mysterious stranger, hot as

fire, gazing back at her—gold beads, red feathers and crimson lipstick. "Where's *your* mask?"

"In here." He removed it from a drawer in the armoire. "It's a stylized version of the Phantom of the Opera."

He put it on. The black mask consisted of bold carvings and flat, smooth pieces of metal, curving around the edges. One side completely covered his face, leaving only his mouth exposed. On the other side, where a small portion of his face was visible, he still wasn't recognizable. He'd been transformed into a mysterious stranger, too, with prominent changes to his forehead, the shape of his eyes and bridge of his nose.

She placed her hand against the section of his jaw that she was able to touch. "I'm going to want you when we come back." She wanted him now, but she wasn't going to start tearing off his tuxedo.

He smiled, much too wickedly. "You're turned on?"

Her skin tingled. "Aren't you?"

His smile turned even more sinful. "You have no idea."

Before they decided to ditch the ball and tumbled into bed, she said, "We better go. You promised Brandon you'd buy some art."

"He's probably counting on me to bid on something no one else will want." He shrugged. "Either that or he's trying to teach me to have some class."

She gave a sputtering laugh. "Can that be taught?"

He laughed it off, too. "Probably not. But let's find out, anyway." He got serious and offered her his arm. "I've already got the limo waiting."

The ball was being held at an elaborate Gothic revival mansion, with architecture that mimicked the icing on top of a wedding cake. Sophie was in awe and thought it was the perfect setting for a masquerade-themed art auction. The proceeds from the fund-raiser were being donated to a wildlife foundation, which factored into the building's motif, as well. Not only was the mansion's decor punctuated with animal prints and faux furs, but the pieces being sold also depicted rare and exotic animals.

Sophie and Tommy wandered the grand halls, trying to hunt down the artwork. All of the pieces were hidden within the house, and there was a treasure map of where to find them. Sophie thought it was a clever tactic, enticing people to uncover whatever they wanted to buy. A security guard was stationed at every treasure site, and to place a bid, guests were required to use a specially designed app they'd downloaded onto their phones.

Other activities included sipping Southern cocktails on the veranda, eating delectable appetizers in the dining room and waltzing to elegant music in the ballroom. There were people everywhere, doing whatever struck their fancies.

Tommy checked the map and pointed in the direction of a narrow staircase that led to the attic. "There's supposed to be a jeweled tiger up there."

Curious, she asked, "What is it, exactly? A painting, a sculpture, a piece of jewelry?"

"I don't know. That's the only description. But the opening bid is pretty high."

She followed him up the staircase, the wood creaking from years of wear.

They entered the attic, which was a steeple-shaped room, cluttered with furniture. They weren't the only people poking around up there. Another masked couple was searching for the tiger, too. But it didn't matter who found it first. Even if they all wanted it, only the highest bidder would win.

The attic was staged to seem as authentic as possible, even if there wasn't a speck of dust in it. The floors were spotless. But you couldn't expect people at a sophisticated ball to crawl around and get dirty.

While Tommy went through some old boxes, Sophie rummaged through a trunk filled with ladies' clothing from the era of the house. If the tiger was a brooch, maybe it would be pinned to one of these dresses.

"I already looked in there," the other woman said to her. "We've been searching everywhere."

Sophie glanced up. Her competitor was a young, slim blonde in a green sequined gown and butterfly-shaped mask.

Sophie politely said, "It's supposed to be in this room."

The blonde knelt beside her. "Maybe he has it on him." She nodded toward the security guard. "Should I frisk him and check?"

Sophie glanced his way. The man was tall and broad, as strong and thick as a live oak. "That's probably not a good idea. He doesn't seem as if he would be receptive to that."

When the guard shot them a stern look, both women clammed up. A second later, they put their masked heads together and giggled like a couple of school-aged kids.

The blonde waited a beat before she stood and smoothed her dress. "There's a hand-carved giraffe my boyfriend is interested in. I think we'll go see if we can find that. Maybe we'll run into you later."

"Sure thing. I'm Sophie, by the way."

A pretty smile appeared on the woman's face. "Jenny." She smiled again. "Good luck with the tiger." She collected her man, and they left the attic.

Soon more people arrived, crowding the small room. By now, Tommy had stopped searching and was gazing out the lone window at the garden below.

Sophie quit sorting through the trunk and went over to him. He turned and leaned into her, then whispered in her ear, "I know where it is."

"Where?" she whispered back.

"Come with me, and I'll show you."

"But—"

He shook his head, silencing her, making her heart

pound. Were they going to leave the attic and return when no one else but the surly guard was there?

Tommy escorted her down the narrow stairs. Once they reached the second floor, they took the main stairwell to the lower level. From there, he whisked her into the backyard.

Was this a ploy to get her alone, to kiss her, to touch her, to leave her breathless for more?

He said, "We need to keep going."

He was taking her to the garden, but she didn't see another living soul around. "I don't think we should be out here."

"It's okay." He threaded his fingers through hers. "There's a lighted path."

They were soft, warm, romantic lights, she thought. "Are you going to seduce me?"

He squeezed her hand. "You bet I am. But not before I show you the tiger."

He led her through a maze of greenery. At least there were flagstones below their feet and they weren't traipsing through the soil. She inhaled a gust of the night air. She wasn't sure if she believed him about the tiger.

Then she saw it: a huge statue in the middle of the garden, surrounded by cottonwoods. Its eyes were amber stones, along with the stripes on its body. A row of floodlights encompassed it, shining up at its muscular frame.

"Oh, my word. Look how big and beautiful it is." She inched closer. "How did you know it was here?"

"When I was looking out the window I caught flashes of gold through the trees, and I realized that the tiger wasn't in the attic, but was visible from it."

"So the map had a trick clue," she concluded, stating the obvious. "There's no one out here to protect it, no security." She reached out to touch one of its legs. "But I guess someone couldn't just cart it away. It would take a crane to lift it. I wonder if anyone else uncovered it yet or if we're the first."

"I don't know. But it's magnificent." He removed his phone from his pocket. "I'm going to place a bid."

"And if you win the bid, then what will you do with it?" She couldn't fathom buying a piece like that, but she didn't have Tommy's money. Or his impulses.

"I'll put it in my garden. I think it'll look as spectacular there as it does here."

He was right—it would. He had plenty of space to accommodate a treasure like this.

When he put his phone away and moved closer to her, she asked, "Is this the part where you seduce me?"

"Not out here, Sophie. We're going back inside, where I can seduce you into kissing me on the dance floor."

Her pulse jumped in her throat. "I told you before that I wasn't going to do that."

"I know. But somewhere deep down, you know you want to."

Heaven forbid, but that was true. She imagined a wicked kiss on the dance floor. "You're right," she said. "I do want to. But I'm glad our identities are hidden." Of course that only added to the mystique, the feeling of the forbidden. "I told Jenny my name, but we're still strangers to her."

He stood in front of the statue, and with the way the floodlights were illuminating him, he looked downright sexy, especially in his mask. "I have no idea who Jenny is."

"The blonde in the attic."

"The other tiger hunter? If you see her again, don't tell her we found it. I want to keep this bad boy to myself."

Sophie wanted to keep her bad boy to herself, too. But suddenly, the thought of their affair ending and him resuming relationships with other women made her uncomfortably possessive. To combat the feeling, she reminded herself that her only concern should be the baby, not hanging on to Tommy. "I'd like to grab a bite before we dance."

"Sure. Let's get something spicy."

She glanced at his mouth. "Appetizers to enhance the taste of our kiss?"

He smiled. "That sounds good to me."

To her, too, she thought. But she didn't reply.

They proceeded to the dining room, and he made up their plates. They ate in silence, indulging in honey chipotle wings, cheesy jalapeño poppers and hot-and-smoky meatballs, then topping it all off with fresh mint ice cream from the dessert bar.

"Are you ready to dance?" he asked, when they finished their last sweet-and-creamy spoonfuls.

"In a second." She set aside her empty bowl, battling a case of nerves. Aside from proper little pecks, she'd never kissed anyone in public.

He fingered the edges of his bow tie. "I can wait as long as you need me to."

She suspected that he was turned on by her hesitation. "How is it that you always seem to get your way?"

He lowered his hand. "You don't have to do this, Sophie."

But she wanted to. Nervous or not, she was too aroused to backpedal. She linked her arm through his, encouraging him to escort her to the ballroom. "I can handle it."

"Yes, ma'am. Whatever you say."

Off they went. Once they arrived on the dance floor, he immediately swept her into a glorious waltz. He moved naturally, easily. But he knew the steps, too. She knew he didn't like these types of events, but apparently he'd learned to waltz just fine.

"I've always wanted to slow-dance with you," he said. "Except in my fantasies, we would be at a honky-tonk bar with a bit more hip action." He softened his voice. "Then again, this is pretty damned nice, too."

Yes, she thought, so incredibly nice. The chandelier above their heads cast a magical glow, giving her the Cinderella vibe again. She leaned in to kiss him. At this point, she just needed to fill her senses.

The taste of him burst on her tongue, causing a tangle of excitement to unfurl in her belly. This could have been their very first kiss, it was so thrilling.

She pressed closer, and as he held her, they kissed some more. Spices and lust, she thought. Cool mint and fiery heat. Sophie moaned, her frilly mask bumping against his.

This was no fairy tale, she thought. This was heat and hunger. She rubbed herself against him, needing more of it.

Finally, she pulled back, putting a proper distance between them. In that reckless instant, she wished that they were at a honky-tonk bar. She'd practically been mauling her date at a charity ball.

She sucked in her breath and peered at the other masked dancers. As far as she could tell, no one was gawking at them. Or gossiping about who they might be or why they were being so ill-behaved. Hadn't anyone noticed that something inappropriate had just happened?

Of course they did, she thought. She just couldn't read the expressions on their masked faces or hear their voices. Besides, at this point, Sophie's mind was fogged. Her skin was still tingling, too. She could barely contain her reactions to Tommy.

"You survived it," he said.

"Yes, I suppose I did." But would this high-society crowd think she was a fool if they uncovered the truth? Would they scorn her for how she was handling this situation? Sooner or later, the public would know. She and Tommy had agreed that once she was good and pregnant, his publicist would announce their news.

His lips curved. "Should we kiss again?"

She glanced at his mouth, and the heat in her belly grew tighter, stronger. But she fought the craving. "I think we should wait until we get home."

"I want to swim naked with you. In my pool, under the waterfalls."

Her mind spun. "Sounds tempting. Do you think we really should?"

He nodded. "It's a great evening for it. The weather is mild, but even if the temperature drops later, it won't matter. I always keep the water warm at this time of year. We can use the pool house to get undressed." He softly added, "Or if you want to let go of all of your inhibitions, we can strip outside and leave our clothes wherever they fall."

Could she do something like that? She didn't know. But for now, she and Tommy were still dancing, swaying in each other's arms.

Until the masquerade was over.

Eight

Tommy was a lucky son of a gun. First he'd gotten Sophie to kiss him at the ball, and now he'd baited her to strip down by the pool. He probably shouldn't be so damn thrilled about corrupting her, though. With the moon shining brightly, she looked like a deer in the headlights, standing there in her pretty little panties and bra.

"What if the bracelet or earrings get lost or damaged?" She grouped them together on a patio table. "They must be terribly expensive, and they're only on loan to you."

"They'll be fine." He was in his underwear, too, and anxious to peel it off and dive into the water. "No one is going to come out here and mess with anything." He'd already notified his staff that the area was off-limits tonight.

She sighed. "I shouldn't be leaving a dress like this draped over a chair. You must have spent a fortune on it, and here we are, treating it like a gunnysack. It's such a beautiful gown, so delicately made. And our masks." She arranged them just so, beside the jewelry.

Tommy wasn't concerned about what happened to their clothes. He didn't even care if the diamonds or garnets she'd worn got lost or damaged. He had enough dough to pay for them, if need be. "I just bought a tiger the size of a tree." He'd won the bid and was having the statue delivered in a few days. "What things cost isn't an issue."

"I know, but…"

"Stop fussing about it." He glanced at the pile of jewelry on the table. "I should have bought it for you, anyway."

She sent him a you're-a-madman look. Then she said, "It's bad enough that I let you pay for the dress. I'm not going to let you turn me into your mistress and start giving me jewelry, too."

"Don't be so dramatic. I've given you expensive gifts before."

"Not jewelry."

"Women make too much of that. Are you ready?" He yanked off his underwear and dived into the pool. He waded in the water, watching her, curious to gauge her reaction before he swam away.

Still wearing her lingerie, she stepped closer to the edge of the pool. "The second waterfall is where your private apartment is. The cave no one except you is allowed to enter."

"I'm going to disengage the alarm, so you can come inside with me." He couldn't explain why he wanted her to share that space with him. He'd built it as his own personal haven, the ultimate man cave. For the most part, Tommy maintained it himself. He didn't have to swim to get there, not unless he wanted to. An elevator on the other side of the pool descended to a water-free entrance, but he rarely used that door.

"What's going on with you?" Sophie asked. "First you're talking about buying me jewelry and now this?"

He smoothed back his wet hair. "I'm probably just feeling macho. I like trying to make you pregnant." He couldn't fathom why else he was behaving this way. "Maybe it'll be lucky for us." Without saying anything else, he submerged himself in the water and swam to his destination.

He dived under the waterfall and reached the cave. Once he was on solid ground, he punched out the numbers on the alarm and went inside.

The first room was merely a place to dry off, with heat lamps and towels. He waited for Sophie there. He was certain that she would find her way.

She appeared a few minutes later, soaking wet in her bra and panties. Little cheat, he thought. But dang, she looked good. Her makeup wasn't even smeared, at least not to the degree of having raccoon eyes. The stylist who'd done her face had probably used the waterproof stuff. Her upswept hairdo was drenched, but given how naturally pretty she was, it only enhanced her appeal.

"Here you go." He wrapped her in a towel and gave her one for her hair, too, which she was already hanging down.

"Thank you." She removed her underwear and dried off. She moved closer to the heat lamps, her damp locks tumbling down her back. "I'm curious to see this private place of yours."

"Sorry, but you're not getting the grand tour. I'm taking you straight to the bedroom."

"Lead the way, then."

Needing no further invitation, he scooped her up and carried her exactly where he wanted to go, passing the living room, kitchen and dining room to get there. The walls throughout the apartment were landscaped with limestone formations. The imperfections pleased him. The furniture, in contrast, was smooth and simple.

"This is quite the cave," she said.

"Yes, it is." No windows, no outside interference, nothing but deliberate solitude.

He'd never wanted to bring anyone here, especially a lover. Sophie was obviously different, somehow. But she'd always been part of his life, so maybe it wasn't so much of a stretch.

He placed her on the bed and followed her down. He didn't hesitate to kiss her. He went full bore, pushing his tongue past her lips. She made sounds of arousal, then arched her back and lifted her hips. He used his hands, playing her like an instrument.

When they stopped kissing, he said, "I really am going to write a song about you."

She gazed curiously at him. "A sexy one?"

"The sexiest." He climbed on top of her. "But I might come up with a ballad, too."

Her breath hitched. "So you're going to write two songs about me?"

"I might do an entire album." At the moment, he wanted to share his feelings for her, send them out into the universe.

"Just don't write any of your phony love songs about me."

He nudged her thighs apart. "Phony?"

She traced rings around his nipples, coiling closer to their flat brown surface, making him feel as if he had jumper cables attached to his body.

"You know what I mean," she said.

Yeah, he knew. Tommy had a poetic side that didn't fit the rest of his personality. She snaked her arms around him, and he entered her, wet and deep.

Together, they made lust-drenched love, holding each other close. The fire between them burned bright. And so did his fascination with her.

She looked mystical, like a mermaid he'd captured at sea. He twined his fingers through her long, ropy hair, grateful that she'd chosen him to sire her child. The more they worked on the baby, the closer he was to making her dreams come true. He'd already gotten his dream of fame and fortune, making music that touched people's souls. He wanted to touch hers, as deeply as he could.

She sighed, and he reached between her legs, rubbing her softly, then with more intensity. She bit her bottom lip and scratched her nails down his back.

When she came, she gasped and shuddered, her breaths warm and silky against his neck. Tommy came, too, his pulse roaring in his ears.

Afterward, they lay side by side, staring up at the rugged limestone ceiling, a languid silence between them. As always, he hoped that he'd made her pregnant. That he'd done his job. But right now, he wasn't going to worry about being the donor and not the dad, and whether the kid would resent him for it. He knew better than to stress about Sophie's baby. She would be parent enough for both of them.

He turned to her and said, "We're still going to skinny-dip later. We didn't actually get to do that."

She shifted onto her side, facing him, as well. "You did."

"Not with you, I didn't. We swam here separately, and you showed up in your bra and panties. I want to see you under the water, bare as the day you were born." He revealed what he'd been thinking about her earlier. "You already remind me of a mermaid."

"So if we swim naked together, I can seem like

one for real?" She wiggled her toes. "Problem is, I don't have a tail."

"That's something I'm willing to overlook."

"You have a lot of fantasies, Tommy."

"When it involves you, I do. I've never obsessed over anyone the way I have over you. Just think of all those years I flirted with you, letting you know how badly I wanted you, while other women were throwing themselves at me."

"That's easy to define."

He frowned. "It is?"

She nodded. "I presented a challenge, and you thrived on the chase."

And he was still chasing her, he realized. "Aside from you, I've always been careful not to go after the ones who might reject me." He didn't put himself in positions of getting hurt. Or having his pride damaged or whatever. "That's hardly anything to brag about."

She flashed a cat-that-ate-the-canary smile. Or maybe she was the canary, devouring the big ol' tomcat.

"You're amused that I'm being humble?" he asked.

"Can you blame me? You're normally so conceited."

"I just pretend to be." He wasn't going to lie, not after the way she'd trapped him with that satisfied smile of hers. "I act more confident than I am."

She squinted, a bit skeptical now, it seemed. "So

you don't really think you're handsome and charming?"

"Well, I wouldn't go that far." He shrugged, making a silly joke. "But in all seriousness, I know I'm a terrible catch and that my inability to commit makes me less desirable."

"I wouldn't be sleeping with you if it wasn't for the baby," she reminded him.

"That just proves how deep our friendship really is." He ran his hands down her body, caressing her, letting her know that he needed her again.

"You're definitely the best friend I've ever had, even if you drive me crazy."

He leaned over her. "Am I driving you nuts now?"

"Absolutely." With a sweet and dreamy sigh, she returned his touch, showing him how much she needed him, too.

After they made love for the second time, Sophie cuddled in Tommy's arms, feeling warm and toasty. Romantic, she thought, like one of the ballads she'd told him not to write about her.

She pressed closer to him. "I shouldn't have said what I did."

He trailed a finger along her spine. "About what?"

"Your ballads being phony. Your slow songs have always been my favorites."

"I'm not offended by what you said. Everyone knows that love isn't my thing. But it's easy for me to write about because I've seen how it affects other people, when they're happy or sad, when it makes them euphoric, when it breaks them. Remember how devastated Conrad was when his wife left him?"

"How could I forget?" His guitar player had nearly lost his mind over his divorce. "But he wasn't faithful to her." She frowned. "I hated being witness to that." Sophie got tired of seeing the infidelities that occurred on the road.

"I try to stay out of the band's personal affairs. But it bothers me when they cheat on their wives and girlfriends, too. It reminds me of how my dad treated my mom, I guess, and that stupid arrangement they had. I never understood how that benefited my mother."

"It didn't, obviously. Especially when Kirby didn't even follow the rules they'd agreed on."

He blew out a breath. "I'm glad Mack has never stepped out on Jean. She's everything to him, her and the kids."

She thought about his drummer and how madly in love he and his wife were. "They definitely have something special." She kept her head on Tommy's shoulder. "Do you think that you shy away from commitment because of the effect your parents' marriage had on you?"

"I don't know. Maybe, probably." He expelled another audible breath. "This is as committed as I've ever been, and it's not even supposed to last."

"*This?* You mean us? Our affair?"

When he nodded, she said, "You're right. It's not supposed to last." But for now, she wanted to make the most of it. She just hoped that she didn't long for him when it was over. That she didn't stay awake at night, pregnant and alone, wondering what he was doing or whom he was with. To keep her mind from straying too far in that direction, she bit playfully at his arm. The last thing she needed was to pine after him, the way she did when they were younger.

He laughed a little. "Why'd you do that?"

"It's your punishment."

"For what?"

"Being so good in bed." And for making her think painful thoughts.

He rolled over on top of her. "Then I should bite you back because you're just as good." He peered into her face. "We should go skinny-dipping now."

"Sure. Why not?" Maybe it would benefit her to jump into the water, to feel it rush over her. "Are we coming back here afterward or going back to your house?"

"Whichever you prefer."

"We'll go back to the house." She didn't want to leave their clothes and masks outside all night. Or the jewels he'd claimed that he should buy her.

"Then let's go." He got up and reached for her hand.

When they left, he reset the alarm, and they stood at the edge of the water, diving in at the same time.

She felt like a mermaid, sleek and smooth and free. Tommy seemed like a merman, too, gliding effortlessly beside her.

They came to the surface, and he swam over to a corner seat at one side of the pool. She followed him, and they shared the space, as close as two beings could be. Naked and wet, they kissed. Taking it a bit further, she crawled onto his lap and made him hard, simply for the fun of it.

After that, they played in the water, splashing and flirting. Once they quieted down, she floated on her back with her hair fanned out around her. Tommy watched her with longing in his eyes.

A short while later they climbed out of the water. He produced a stack of towels and two thick robes from the pool house, and they dried off and bundled up.

"Did skinny-dipping with me live up to your fantasy?" she asked, as they prepared to gather their belongings and return to the mansion.

"Oh, yeah." He grinned boyishly, happily. "It definitely did."

She thought about her bad-girl fantasy and her desire to be watched. She'd convinced herself that she was too shy to do it. But there was a part of her that desperately wanted to. If she told Tommy how she felt, would he be shocked? No doubt it would arouse the hell out of him. But she kept quiet. She just wasn't ready to go there.

Nonetheless, she was still feeling sleek and sexy. She grabbed a hold of him, and they kissed with heat and vigor. They even slipped their hands into each other's robes, feeling for whatever flesh they could find.

Would they ever stop wanting each other?

Of course they would, the practical side of Sophie's mixed-up mind answered. Just as soon as she was pregnant and their skyrocketing affair came crashing back to earth.

A week after the masquerade ball, Sophie returned from the office and changed into comfortable clothes. She loved being home by five thirty and kicking back for the rest of the night. Overall, she appreciated her new job and enjoyed assisting Tommy's manager. Sophie already knew how to run a tour, and now Barbara was teaching her more about advertising, marketing and the financial end of the business. She'd had a particularly interesting day today. While they were going over current contracts and negotiations, Barbara informed her about a highly lucrative reality-show deal that Tommy was refusing to consider.

Funny, but he'd never even mentioned it to Sophie. Clearly, he didn't tell her everything that pertained to his career...or his personal life, for that matter. She was still learning new things about him. Especially sexual things, she thought. She certainly knew his bedroom preferences now.

As for herself, her voyeuristic fantasy was getting stronger. Should she do it? The idea of being really, really bad thrilled her. But she was still grappling with the self-consciousness of it.

Clearing her mind, she made her way to the kitchen and opened the fridge. Chef knew that she liked to nib-

ble between meals and always had something ready
for her. If he wasn't there to give the food directly to
her, he wrote her name on the containers.

Just as Sophie turned around, Dottie entered the
kitchen, with her twinkling blue eyes and short graying hair.

She smiled and said, "I see you found what Chef
left for you."

"I did, indeed." He'd been spoiling Sophie since
the day she moved in, and she adored him for it. Chef
Bryan was a quiet man, in his late fifties, with a shiny
bald head and a heart of gold. "Where is he, anyway?"

"He left early today. He has a date."

"Really?" Instantly intrigued, Sophie wondered
more about it. She'd always been interested in other
people's love lives. When she was a teenager, she used
to document her friends' experiences in her diary and
then read them her entries to see if they approved.
She never wrote down who Tommy went out with,
though. She hadn't wanted to put his conquests on
paper or discuss them with him. "I didn't know Chef
was seeing someone."

"It's his first time meeting her. They connected on
an online dating site. For older folks." Dottie made a
goofy face. "Tommy is going to send someone out for
pizza tonight. That's what he decided to have since
Chef isn't here."

That sounded good to Sophie. "Where is Tommy?"
She hadn't seen him since she'd come home.

"In his studio. But he should be taking a break

soon. He has your dogs with him. They were with me earlier, but he nabbed them. Hokey and Pokey are such characters."

"Yes. They're a couple of rascals." They dashed around the mansion as if they owned the place, and Tommy indulged them as if they did.

Dottie leaned closer. "So, what type of snack did Chef prepare for you?"

"I don't know. I haven't peeked inside yet." Sophie lifted the lid and poked around. "Cheese, crackers, artichoke dip, roasted chickpeas, turkey-and-cucumber roll-ups. Good, healthy things. Oh, and look, he included ants on a log. I told him they were my favorite when I was little. That my dad used to fix them for me, and now Chef made them for me, too."

"That's so nice. He catered my niece's birthday party and made the most adorable appetizers. Not just ants on a log, but butterflies, caterpillars and snails, too. He used celery sticks and peanut butter with crackers and fruit and pretzels to create them. He also made apple bites that looked like happy-faced monsters and desserts the kids could decorate themselves."

Sophie imagined him catering her child's parties, too. "How old is your niece?"

"Five. She's my grandniece, actually. My sister's spunky little granddaughter." Dottie removed her phone from her pocket and flashed a photo of a freckle-faced girl with a gap-toothed grin. "Her name is Kelly."

"She's darling." Sophie smiled. "As cute as can be."

"I think so, too, but I'm biased. I got her a trampoline for her birthday. It's what she wanted. Thank goodness it has a safety net around it." Dottie sighed and stepped back, rolling her neck and arching her back. "I'm about ready to quit for the day and put my feet up."

Sophie nodded. Dottie lived on the premises and had been managing Tommy's household since her husband died. She'd never had any children, and hence had no grandchildren of her own, either. She needed to be commended for taking such good care of Tommy, even if she didn't always approve of his lifestyle.

"You do a wonderful job around here," Sophie said.

"Thank you, honey. That means a lot coming from you. Now go and enjoy your snacks."

"I think I'll eat in the garden and visit the tiger Tommy bought."

Dottie laughed. "At least it's only a statue. Be sure to text him in case he wants to see you on his break. Otherwise he'll be searching high and wide for you."

"I will." Sophie grabbed a bottle of water and exited the kitchen through a back door. She took the grassy path to the garden. The weather was starting to cool off a bit, but not enough to need a jacket. At least not right now. In an hour or so, it could get breezy.

She parked herself on the bench in front of the tiger

and texted Tommy. He didn't reply, so she munched on her goodies. While she was on her second turkey-and-cucumber roll-up, her phone signaled a text. Tommy was on his way to see her.

When he appeared, he looked downright dreamy, rugged to the core, in crisp denims and battered cowboy boots.

"Sophie-Kophie," he said and sat next to her. "How are you?"

"I'm good. So where are my dogs? Dottie said they were with you."

"They're asleep in my studio. They were watching animal videos on the internet earlier."

She raised her eyebrows, picturing it in her mind. "They chose what to watch all by themselves?"

He shrugged. "I might have had a hand in it."

"No doubt." She offered him the snack box. "Are you hungry?"

"I'll take a few of those." He picked through the roasted chickpeas. He eyeballed the ants on a log and grinned. "What are you, in kindergarten again?"

She defended herself. "I can't help it if Chef babies me."

"Everyone loves having you here. They're never going to want you to leave."

With the way things were going, she was afraid that she was never going to want to leave, either. But she was still trying to get pregnant, so there was no need to rush. When the time came, she would quit obsessing about being Tommy's live-in lover and return to her own home. She mulled over the way she'd phrased it. *Live-in lover.* It sounded so real. But it wasn't. Not with how temporary it was.

He took another handful of the legumes. "How was work today?"

"Funny you should ask." She paused to regroup her thoughts. "Barbara told me about *Music Mentors* and how badly they want you to do the show. I don't understand why you're not considering it."

"Because I'd have to commit to two years of being a mentor and hold off on touring on my own. Then I'd have to tour with my protégés as my opening acts, with the show controlling the whole thing."

"Yes, but they book some exceptional tours. Besides, I think you'd enjoy scouring clubs for up-and-coming artists to mentor. You'd have a lot of clout in that regard. You'd get to pick your protégés yourself. And your segments would be filmed right here in Nashville."

"I agree that it would be nice to help new acts make it in this business. But doing television would still be too much of a commitment for me. I need more freedom than that."

"Then I guess there's no point in discussing it. But the amount of money they're offering you is staggering. More than anyone else who's ever been on the show." Tommy had the perfect personality for reality TV and the producers obviously knew it.

He shrugged. "I should get back to my studio."

"Okay. Then I'll see you later for pizza."

"So you know about that, huh? Chef taking the rest of the day off for a date? Speaking of which, I haven't kissed you since this morning." He homed in on her, putting his face wonderfully close to hers.

Her heart pounded with excitement. After he kissed her, she decided that she was going to unleash her fantasy. This very evening. With him. No holds barred. She was going to make it happen.

At this point, there was no reason to put it off. She had a right to explore her sexuality, to become her own woman.

She said, "I'm going to give you a thrill tonight."

He touched her cheek. "You always thrill me, Soph."

"I'm capable of thrilling you even more." Dizzying as this feeling was, she liked the power it gave her. "But you'll have to wait to see what I mean. And you'll have to say 'please.'"

He furrowed his brow. "Even if I don't know what I'm saying it for?"

"Yes." Him not knowing made it more exciting for her. She needed this. She really, truly did. "When we were younger, you used to make me say 'pretty please with five pounds of sugar on top' when I wanted something from you. But you didn't always give in."

"I'm giving in now." He lowered the tone of his voice. "How about 'pretty please with all of the sugar in the world on top'?"

She couldn't help but smile. "Then what choice do I have?" She was going to fulfill her own fantasy, giving him a night to remember, too.

Nine

At bedtime, Tommy waited for Sophie to get undressed, but she stayed in her jeans and blouse. She'd told him to keep what he had on, too. So he stood there, fully clothed and thoroughly confused.

Ignoring him for now, she moved two chairs from his dining alcove to the center of the bedroom. She placed them across from each other, but not too close, leaving a purposeful span between them. Earlier she'd promised that she was going to give him a thrill, and he was intrigued by the mystery of it all.

"That's your chair." She pointed to the one on the right. "And that's mine." She gestured to the second seat.

He noticed that hers was in shadow. "What should I do now?"

"Just sit and behave."

If he weren't so fascinated by whatever she was planning, he might've laughed. She was being adorably bossy. He parked his butt in the chair. "Can I at least take off my boots?"

"No."

"Why not?"

"Because they're sexy, and I like how you look in them."

He thought they were old and dusty, but who was he to argue?

She roamed her gaze over him, assessing him in ways he couldn't begin to understand. Then she said, "Open your legs some more."

He was already slouched in a wide-legged spread. But he wasn't foolish enough to protest. He followed her order. Nonetheless, he asked, "Is there a reason I have to sit this way?"

"Other than me enjoying seeing you that way? No, there isn't."

Tommy shivered all the way to his battered boots. "Can I unzip my jeans to alleviate the pressure?" By now, he was getting hard.

She shook her head. "I'll unzip them for you later."

"You're making me suffer, Soph." But he liked it, and was eager for whatever came next.

She took her seat. "This is nice, isn't it?"

"If *nice* is another word for *hot*, then, yeah, this is the nicest thing anyone has ever done to me." He could barely breathe. He'd never had a woman torture him this way.

"Just so you know, this is my fantasy, Tommy. Something I always imagined, something forbidden I always wanted to do. But it's also something you told me that you like your lovers to do."

His brain kicked into gear. Suddenly he knew; he understood. "I'm going to watch you."

"Yes." She removed her bra without even taking off her blouse. She simply maneuvered her arms, pulling it out from beneath the hem.

He was impressed by her slick move. She was definitely giving him a thrill, making good on her promise.

She dropped her bra onto the floor. Her nipples were poking against her blouse. He'd heard that women's areolas sometimes got darker with pregnancy. He wondered if that would happen to her.

"I'm not taking my jeans off," she said. "I'm just going to…" She opened the zipper and tugged them down, just enough to expose her panties.

Tommy let out the breath he'd been holding. Her panties consisted of multicolored lace and a cute little bow. She slipped her hand past the waistband, and he feared he would lose his mind.

She moved her hand, sliding it lower. He watched her, bewitched by her modesty, by how sweet and sensual she was. Everything about her turned him on: the way she nibbled on her bottom lip, the dreamy expression in her eyes, the cascade of her unbound hair.

She rubbed gently, touching herself ever so lightly.

"Is that how you always do it?" he asked. "Softly like that?"

"Yes," she responded breathlessly.

"Have you ever thought about me when you were doing it?"

"Yes," she said again. "More times than I can count."

"You look beautiful." So damn gorgeous, he thought.

"Maybe I can…" She pulled her jeans farther down. She tugged her panties lower, too.

Now Tommy could see the top of her mound. She was getting braver, letting some of her modesty go. He couldn't take his eyes off her.

"Come for me, Sophie," he whispered. "Come while I'm watching you."

She peeked at him through drowsy eyelids. She looked stoned, high on seducing him. He was hooked, that was for sure.

She opened her legs, caught her breath and rocked in her seat. She kept touching herself; it was perfection in every way. So hot. So erotic.

Tommy studied every move she made.

When she came, her orgasm was a thing of beauty, of sugar and spice and everything nice. Now that word made complete sense.

Nice, nice, nice.

Fixated on the sweet sounds she made, he absorbed her emotions, taking them deep inside.

She sighed and removed her hand from her panties.

He waited until her eyes were less glazed before he said, "That was incredible. Thank you for letting me be part of it."

Her smile was rife with sensuality. "I needed to make that happen, to free my inhibitions. But now it's your turn to feel good."

"I'm already feeling good." He was still mesmerized by her.

"Then it's your turn to feel even better." She stood and righted her clothes. "This is part of my fantasy, too." She got on her knees in front of him, and their gazes locked.

Desperate to touch her, he caressed her face. Silent, she undid his jeans and freed him, his desire more than evident.

When she lowered her head and took him in her mouth, everything went blank, except the mindless pleasure she gave him.

Tommy and Sophie spent the next two weeks working on the baby, doing what they were meant to do. And now he waited nervously outside the bathroom door. Sophie's cycle was four days late, and she was taking a pregnancy test. According to the instructions, this test could be taken as early as one day after a missed period. Bearing that in mind, he figured that four days was plenty of time for an accurate reading.

As soon as the door clicked open and she emerged, he anxiously asked, "What did it say?"

"It says that we did it, Tommy! I'm going to have a baby!" She squealed and leaped into his arms.

He spun her around, like they were kids on a carousel. He couldn't remember being this excited, not even when he'd gotten his first number one hit. Lord almighty, but nothing compared to creating a life. An embryo in her womb, he thought. A teeny, tiny speck that would develop into a human being. Amazing how something so minuscule could be so monumental.

They stopped spinning and broke into laughter. Sophie was going to be a mommy. She was going to have the child she wanted so badly.

A second later, they went warmly, sweetly quiet. He lifted her T-shirt and splayed a hand across her stomach.

Her eyes glistened with tears. "Thank you for doing this for me."

"You're welcome." He poked her belly button, proud and awed that he'd become a successful donor. He couldn't imagine what being an actual dad would be like.

But then he stopped himself; that wasn't part of the plan. Tommy being the father wasn't in the baby's best interest. Still, he couldn't help but wonder if he would be as terrible at it as he first thought. Not that it mattered. This was Sophie's baby. He'd signed a contract that absolutely, positively said so. Besides, he was just feeling all good and manly about making her pregnant. And that had nothing to do with being a parent.

"So what happens now?" he asked.

She stepped back, out of his arms. "I'll call my doctor and make an appointment to see him."

That was the logical answer, but he was thinking on a more personal level. "Is it okay to tell my family? Or Dottie or Chef Bryan? And what about Barbara? You work with her every day."

"We can tell the people we're closest to, but I don't want the public to know. It's too early for that. I want to be at least twelve weeks along before we make a formal announcement. The first trimester is the most precarious, and I don't want to jinx it."

He didn't like the sound of that. "Maybe you shouldn't go back home right away. It'd probably be better if you stayed here."

"I'll be fine, Tommy."

"I know. But it just seems safer." He would worry if she was by herself. "Plus, I'd like to see how you're progressing each day. I'd be glad to go to your doctor appointments with you, if you don't mind the company."

"Really?" She sounded surprised by his offer, but appreciative, too. "Thank you. I'd like that."

He made another offer, a riskier one, this time. "You can keep sleeping in my room."

She blinked at him. "But our affair was supposed to end when I got pregnant."

"I realize that's what we agreed on. But it doesn't have to be over this soon, not if we're both still enjoying it." He wasn't ready to let her go just yet, and he hoped she wasn't ready to be rid of him, either. He just wanted a little more time together.

She met his gaze. "I do enjoy it."

"I do, too." So damn much, he thought. "So should we keep at it?"

Her breath rushed out. Was she going to agree? Or would she decide to stick to their original plan and go back home by herself? He waited, hoping her decision would go in his favor.

Finally she said, "I'll stay." They gazed silently at each other, and she hurriedly added, "But once I'm farther along, after this first trimester is over, I'll go home and that will be the end of it. Does that work for you?"

"Yes, of course." He wasn't expecting anything more. "I'm going to try to get back on the road later, anyway. I'm still hoping to add some dates to this latest tour."

"You better hurry up and hire a road manager to replace me." She paused. "Or have you found someone already?"

"No, not yet. But I will." He teased her. "You just keep sidelining me."

She smiled. "Me and my zest for motherhood?"

"Yep." He drew her into his arms again, holding her close and resting his hand on her stomach, where her baby was destined to grow.

The next morning, Sophie sat across from Tommy on the balcony, picking at her breakfast. She'd barely slept a wink the night before. Was she doing the right thing by remaining at his house? By sleeping with him? A less attached woman would have returned to her own home, her own life, her own everything.

Moving the eggs around on her plate, she glanced up at him. What if she didn't want to leave later? What if she started craving a real relationship with Tommy, something committed, something long and lasting and deep? She would be in major trouble if that happened.

"Do you think you're going to be sick?" he asked.

She stilled her fork. "I'm sorry. What?"

"Do you think you're going to get morning sickness and all of that?"

"I don't know. Most women do, I guess. But there should be ways to alleviate it. I'll talk to my doctor about it, just in case." She studied him in the overcast light. The clouds blocked the sun, creating a hazy ambience.

He refreshed his coffee from the carafe on the table. She was drinking herbal tea. She knew that caffeine wasn't good for pregnant women.

"When are you going to call your doctor?" he asked.

"Today, as soon as his office opens. I'm hoping they can get me in within the next few days. But maybe it would be better if you didn't go with me to any of my appointments."

Tommy frowned. "Why not?"

Because having him there might make her feel

even closer to him, and she was already struggling with those feelings. "I think it'll create some problems." In all sorts of ways, she thought. "You're too famous to walk into my doctor's office without anyone recognizing you. And since it's an OB-GYN, it might make people wonder what you're doing there. Another patient might snap a picture of you and Tweet about it. And then the media will start speculating, and our plan to keep this under wraps could fall to pieces."

His frown deepened. "So we'll arrange to go through a private entrance like I do with my doctor."

"I don't want anyone making special allowances for me. Besides, it could still turn into a three-ring circus if someone on the nursing staff is a fan of yours." She knew how giddy people got in his presence, especially the young, crush-crazed types.

"You didn't have a problem with this last night."

"I was caught up in the moment. But now I'm thinking a bit more clearly." Or she was trying to, anyway.

"I understand that having to deal with my celebrity can get overwhelming. But it doesn't have to be the three-ring circus you talked about." He leaned forward in his chair. "I can get you your own private physician, and he or she can come to the house. You can have your appointments right here."

"Oh, my goodness, Tommy. That's way too much. I want to see my own doctor in his own office. And I want to do it by myself."

He expelled a hard sigh. "All right. But when we announce that I'm your baby's donor, you're still going to have to cope with the media side of this."

"I know. But I'll be geared up for it by then. Plus, I won't be living here anymore. I'll be at my house, and you'll be working toward getting back on the road." They would be separate entities. Or at least that was the plan.

He sent her a concerned look. "You're not having second thoughts about staying here now, are you?"

Yes, she most definitely was. But she didn't want to bring her fears to his attention. Nothing would be worse than falling in love with him. She knew what a disaster that would be. Yet even as panicked as she was, she wasn't ready to give him up completely.

"Are you?" he persisted.

"Am I what?" she replied, confused.

"Having second thoughts about staying here for the next twelve weeks?"

"No," she lied. But with any luck, she would be prepared to part ways with him by then.

"I'm really glad you're going to stay." A devilish smile spread across his face. "You're as beautiful as ever, Soph. Sexy, too. Pregnancy suits you."

She clucked her tongue, playing down his desire. "You say that now, but you're not going to think I'm sexy when my hormones kick into gear."

"Nothing is going to change how hot you are to me. Now, get over here, little mama, and climb onto my lap." He patted his thighs for effect, flirting shamelessly with her.

Was it wrong that she liked him calling her "little mama"? Or that she wanted him as badly as he appeared to want her? She gave up the fight and flirted with him, too. "I'm not going to bump and grind with you over breakfast. But if you sit perfectly still, I might come over there and give you a long, luscious kiss."

He flexed his hands. "I won't move, I promise."

She left her seat and scooted onto his lap, looping her arms around his neck. He groaned, and she kissed him soft and deep. When she broke her lips away from his, he nuzzled her cheek.

"So is there anything new going on with you?" she asked. "Besides making your best friend pregnant?"

"Ha ha. Funny lady. Actually, I've been thinking about going to Texas to see Matt. And I'd love for you to join me. If your doctor says it's all right for you to travel, do you want to go? Maybe even this weekend?"

"Oh, wow. Really? That soon?" She'd spent a portion of her life being on the road with Tommy, and now he was suggesting a quick getaway. But maybe a little vacation would be a nice change of pace. "I'll check with my doctor. But I'm sure it won't be a problem. Pregnant women travel all the time."

"I'll need to call Matt to arrange it, but he told me before that I could visit anytime. It'll certainly be a lot more fun having you there, sharing the experience with me. Since Libby has been going back and forth and is returning to Texas this weekend, we could offer her a seat on my plane with the three of us making the trip together."

"I like that idea. It would be good for you to get to know your brother better." And Sophie could get to know Libby better, too. With everything that had been going on, they hadn't seen each other since the picnic at Kirby's.

"Then it's a date." He rocked her gently, keeping her on his lap. "Since it's a recreational ranch, there will be plenty of things for us to do. The weather is nice at this time of year, too." He paused and added, "Of course, for now we can't reveal that I'm Matt's brother. But Matt and I already have a cover story, where we'll just say that we're friends."

She understood that they were protecting Matt's identity until the book came out. Just as Sophie was protecting the secret of her pregnancy until she was further along.

But the biggest thing she needed to protect was her heart, and keep it far, far away from Tommy.

Sophie was used to flying on Tommy's private jet. It was the same plane he used when he toured. At the moment, he was kicking back in one of the bedrooms, and Sophie and Libby sat side by side in the main compartment.

"This is so luxurious," Libby said, with her big blue eyes all aglow. "Up until now, I've been taking commercial flights. Kirby pays for me to travel first class, though, so I can't complain."

"How's the book coming?" Sophie asked, curious about the process.

"I'm working on the rough draft, so it's moving along. I still have a few more interviews to conduct, but I can fill those areas in later." Libby tucked a strand of her wavy blond hair behind her ear. "I still need to talk to you and Tommy about the details of your donor agreement and how much of it you're comfortable sharing in the book."

"We can discuss all of that this weekend. It won't really matter because by the time the book comes out the news will be public knowledge anyway." At that point, Sophie would have gotten used to people knowing who her baby's donor was.

"Yes, but it's important for me to tell it in the way you and Tommy want it to be told. For example, do you want me to disclose the fact that you're together?"

Sophie's heart bumped inside her chest. "We won't be together by then." Libby obviously knew that Sophie and Tommy were lovers. Kirby probably told her, maybe even in reference to the book since that seemed to be a concern of Libby's. "Me moving in with Tommy was just a temporary arrangement while I became pregnant. I'll be staying just a bit longer now, but it's still going to end."

The blonde flashed a dimpled smile. "Are you sure about that? If it was a regular donor situation, you wouldn't have been together to begin with, and now that you're pregnant, you're still together. That seems more like a relationship than a business arrangement to me."

"It isn't." Sophie defended the absurdity of remaining Tommy's bedmate. "I'm only staying with him through my first trimester. Then I'll be going home."

"And you'll stop…sharing a bed?"

"Yes, definitely." She tried to sound less worried than she was. She didn't want to admit that she had fears about falling in love with him.

Libby shifted in her seat. She sat near the window, with clouds floating by. "I hope I'm not meddling, but I think you'd make a great couple."

Sophie shook her head, trying to keep calm. This wasn't a conversation she'd expected to have. "It just seems that way because Tommy and I are such close friends."

"Yes, but that's what gives you the background for developing a relationship. And it's obvious how strong your chemistry is."

Determined to lessen the significance of their attraction, she waved her hand, brushing it off. "That'll go away."

"Really? How? Just by willing it away? Matt and I tried to have a no-strings affair and now look at us."

Engaged and raising a family together? None of that applied to Sophie. "It's different for me and Tommy. We only got together so I could have my baby. I never would have been with him otherwise. He's just too much of a player."

"I'm aware of Tommy's history. But he doesn't seem that way now that he's with you."

"That's just an illusion." A magic trick, she thought. "He'll go back to his old ways when the newness of what we're doing wears off."

"I guess you know his patterns better than anyone."

"Yes, I do." She knew how flighty he could be, how easily distracted, and she couldn't imagine him being any other way. "Besides, I'm not interested in having him as my partner." She knew better than to want the impossible.

"Okay. But if things get complicated, and you ever need someone to talk to, I'm a good listener."

"Thank you. That's sweet. But I'm fine with how things are." Or so she kept telling herself.

Either way, she didn't think that Libby believed her. Matt's fiancée seemed to know that Sophie was struggling with her feelings. She just hoped that Tommy didn't figure it out, too.

Ten

The Flying Creek Ranch was a magnificent place. Sophie loved the layout of the land and the vast beauty of the Texas Hill Country. Some of the regular activities included horseback riding, hayrides, hiking, swimming, fishing, skeet shooting, campfires, barn dances, horseshoes and Ping-Pong.

Matt insisted that they stay at his house instead of in one of the guest cabins or at the main lodge. The single-story, custom-built home he shared with Libby and Chance was beautifully crafted, big and woodsy with stone floors.

Sophie had already gotten a glimpse of the three of them together at Kirby's, but seeing them here in their own environment was even more compelling.

But that wasn't the half of it. Tommy's interaction with Chance was really doing a number on her.

She stood in the doorway of the den and watched them from across the expansive room. Tommy was playing a video game with Chance and getting along brilliantly with the boy. Typically Tommy didn't click with children; it wasn't his forte. But soon after they'd arrived, six-year-old Chance started following Tommy around like a wolf cub, drawing him into the kid zone.

Dang it, Sophie thought. She was already worried about falling in love with Tommy, and this wasn't helping. Still, it made her heart glad to know that he was honing his kid skills.

Nonetheless, Chance was kicking his ass in the game. Funny, too, because it was a rodeo game and Tommy could ride mechanical bulls like nobody's business. The virtual ones? Apparently, not so much. But he was still enjoying himself. He laughed every time he screwed up, with Chance ribbing him along the way.

Libby came up beside Sophie and whispered, "They're cute together."

"Yes, they are." She spoke quietly, too. "So cute, so sweet." But she was trying not to get sucked too deeply into it, at least not where it would knock her into a lovesick abyss. "This is the first time Tommy has bonded with a child."

"Then I'm glad it could be with Chance."

"So am I." She moved away from the door, making sure their conversation remained private. Libby followed her down the hall and Sophie said, "You'd never know it by the way Tommy is playing that game, but he's an incredible cowboy. We already talked about him teaching my child to ride and rope. When we were kids, he helped me be a better cowgirl."

"Your relationship with him is really special—to be such close friends for so many years. You did right by choosing him as your donor."

"Thank you. It's important for me to hear you say that." Especially since Sophie was in a state of emotional distress. "I'm not doing as well as I let on earlier." At this point it didn't make sense to pretend, not when Libby already appeared to sense the truth. "But I'm sure you figured me out."

"I can tell how Tommy affects you." She put her hand on Sophie's arm. "He has a powerful presence."

"I'm afraid of falling in love with him." She couldn't bear to need more from him than he was capable of giving. She would never recover from the problems it would cause.

"I understand how daunting your concerns must be. But maybe in time loving him will seem like a good thing."

"I hope so." Because for now just the thought alone made her ache.

On Saturday night, a barn dance was under way. But at the moment, Tommy sat next to Matt at a rustic wooden table, away from the crowd. They'd already eaten a country-fried meal, and now Libby, Sophie and Chance were line dancing, leaving the men by themselves.

Tommy's celebrity had caused a stir, but he didn't mind. Earlier, he'd taken tons of selfies with other guests and signed cocktail napkins and whatever else they gave him to scribble on.

He'd made nice with the cover band, too. He'd sat in on a couple of old country tunes with them. He'd also offered to Tweet a link to a YouTube video that featured their original material. Overall, they were a damn fine group of musicians, talented in their own right.

Tommy checked out the line dancers. Chance was doing what he could to keep up, but he missed most of the steps, turning the wrong way nearly every time.

Amused, Tommy said to Matt, "You need to teach that pint-size cowboy to dance."

His half brother chuckled. "I'm working on it. But dancing doesn't come easy to him. He's a hell of a roper, though."

"That's what I've heard. He's a great kid. Being around him is making me more excited about the baby Sophie is going to have. It's still really early, but it's kind of cool to touch her stomach and know there's a little peanut in there."

Matt picked up his beer. "So you're going to call it Peanut Talbot?"

Tommy laughed. A second later, he realized that he had no idea what Sophie was going to call her child. They hadn't discussed what her choices might be. But to make things clear, he said, "It'll be more like Peanut Cardinale. It'll have Sophie's surname." That much he did know.

"Oh, of course. Sorry. I have my mom's last name, too."

Tommy nodded. "Are she and her husband going to stop by the dance tonight?" Matt's mom lived on the ranch with a man she'd recently married.

"They should be here soon. She's interested in meeting you."

"I guess it's only fair since you met my mom." It was strange, too, to think about the way their mothers had catered to their father back in the day, giving Kirby whatever he wanted. "What's on your birth certificate? Who's named as the father?"

"It says 'unknown.' Whenever anyone asked about him, I'd just say that he was a drifter and that my mom never even knew his real name. But that's what I was instructed to say." Matt set down his half-empty beer. "When Kirby first started coming around, I didn't know he was my dad. Eventually I sensed it, though. And then my mom told me the truth."

"At least it didn't take you by surprise. That must have made it a little easier."

"Yeah, I suppose it did. Is your name going to be on the birth certificate for Sophie's kid?"

"No. But we're still going to tell him or her who I am."

"It sounds like you have it all worked out."

"We certainly tried to." Tommy glanced at Sophie, thinking how natural she looked in this setting. A moment later, something inside him went tight—he felt a sudden fear about how easily she could shut him out of her child's life. Of course, that was a stupid thing to think about. Why would Sophie do that to him? He wasn't going to contest their agreement or try to be the dad. Yet Sophie seemed different now that she was pregnant. More cautious, he thought. He even got the sinking feeling that their friendship could be on the line. And if Sophie stopped being friends with him, then he wouldn't get to see the child, either. He would be left out in the cold.

"There's my mom," Matt said suddenly, interrupting Tommy's mental ramblings.

He turned and saw an attractive fiftysomething brunette heading toward them. As for her husband, he was tall and lanky, fair-skinned, with thinning gray hair and a kind face. He already knew that their names were Julie and Lester.

Soon Sophie, Libby and Chance joined them at the table, and they spent the rest of the evening together. Chance dashed over to the buffet and brought back a huge slice of apple pie. When Sophie caught sight of it, she went and got some, too, and with the way she moaned over its cinnamon flavor, Tommy wondered if she was having her first pregnancy food craving.

She offered him a bite but he refused, not wanting to take it away from her and the little peanut he'd planted in her womb.

After the dance, Tommy lay next to Sophie in the guest room they were sharing, staring up at the ceiling. The bed was warm, the covers smooth against his skin. Outside the window, the night sky was sprinkled with stars.

He leaned onto his elbow, shifting to look at her. "How long will it be before you know if it's a boy or a girl?"

She turned in his direction. "Between four and five months, I think. I didn't really talk to my doctor about that. I don't even have to go back to see him for another six weeks. That's when my prenatal visits will start."

Tommy wouldn't know anything about that, considering that she'd banned him from going with her. "When are you going to start thinking up names? Are you going to wait until you know if it's a boy or a girl? Or are you going to start playing with ideas now?"

"I don't know. I haven't gotten that far."

He wouldn't mind if she involved him in the process, but with the way things were going, that seemed doubtful. "It wouldn't hurt to start making a list."

"I suppose I could do that." She adjusted the covers, loosening them around her body. "Chance's name certainly suits him, with the whole outlaw thing from your dad's song."

"Chance does seem like a little wilding. Your kid will probably be that way, too, with my blood running through its veins."

She placed her hand on her stomach. "I'll bet it'll kick up a storm in my belly."

He wanted to cover her hand with his, but he kept his paws to himself. "I've taken to calling it Peanut."

"Really?" She glanced up and smiled. "Oh, that's so cute."

"It's probably a common nickname, but it's what jumped into my mind. After the way you devoured that apple pie tonight, maybe I should be calling it Seedling."

She laughed. "I did chow down. But gosh, it was good. I'm still partial to Peanut, though." She paused. "Here's something I could consider—if it's a boy, I could use my dad's name for its middle name, and if it's a girl, I could use my mom's."

"Sure. Why not?" He appreciated her bouncing her ideas off of him. "That would be a nice way to honor your parents."

Her voice turned low, soft and sad. "I wish they were here."

"I know. I'm sorry." Tommy had been a pallbearer at her father's funeral. But her mom had always been a bit of a mystery to him. Since she'd died so soon after Sophie was born, he didn't really know much about her. "Do you think it'll be okay for you to just have one kid?"

"What do you mean?"

"Being an only child seems like it would be lonely."

"It was a little lonely for me. But I had you to hang out with, so that helped." She angled her head. "Are you offering to be the donor of my second child, if I ever decided to have another one? Because I thought you were getting a vasectomy after this one is born."

"Truthfully, I don't know what I'm saying or doing or offering. I'm kind of mixed up tonight. I got a little worried while we were at the dance."

"About what?"

"How easily you could shut me out of the kid's life." He tried to make sense of the insecurity churning inside him. "But I think some of this might be coming from how it hurts that you don't want me going to the doctor with you."

"I already explained why—"

"I know. But it just makes me realize how much control you have over this situation. It even feels like a blow to our friendship, and since us being friends is my only connection to the child, it makes me being the donor more difficult, too."

"I don't mean to make you feel that way." She hesitated, closing her eyes, keeping them tightly shut. A second later, she opened them and said, "I'm just trying to cope with everything, too."

Of course she was, he thought. This was a whole new experience for her, as well. "Don't worry about it, Soph. I shouldn't have even brought it up. We came here to have a nice getaway, and I'm ruining it." He reached for her. "Just forget I said anything."

She nuzzled against him. "You're still my friend, Tommy." She trailed a hand down his body, her touch sensuously familiar. "You're still my lover, too."

That was all the invitation he needed. He rolled on top of her, kissing her, tasting the heat of her lips. She sighed, and he lifted the hem of her nightgown. It was a delicate garment, as white as a wedding gown and just as lacy.

Before he thought too deeply about that, he raised the material even higher. She was bare underneath, and he was already naked.

She parted her thighs, and he slid between them, getting an immediate sense of belonging. But being inside her always affected him in that way.

He thrust slowly, his body rocking hers. She whispered something incoherent in his ear. Which was understandable, especially on a scattered night such as this. He'd already created an uncomfortable situation, that was for sure.

Silent, he focused on making her feel good, sweeping her into a sea of sensation, where nothing else was supposed to matter.

Except the comfort of sex.

On their last evening at the ranch, Sophie and Tommy went on a hayride in a straw-filled horse-drawn wagon. They were part of a caravan, en route to a campfire and marshmallow roast. They rode with Matt and Libby and Chance, and the boy chattered the entire way.

Sophie enjoyed listening to him. He was being their tour guide, telling them about the scenery and the colorful glass bottles hanging from the trees. Most of the bottles were blue because Matt was a Cherokee from the "Blue Clan." It was obvious that Chance was repeating things Matt had told him, but he did it with such love and admiration, it made Sophie smile.

Libby interjected and said, "The first time I took this ride with Matt, we were alone, just the two of us, and gazing up at the stars. But since neither of us knows much about the constellations, we made up names for them."

Sophie could tell that Libby was reminiscing about an early memory with Matt, a night of romance. Or maybe it had been during a time when they'd been longing for love and fighting their feelings for each other.

Sophie was certainly battling her feelings for Tommy. Nothing had changed in that regard. She stole a jittery glance at him while he was looking the other way. Last night he'd shared his concerns with her, and tonight they were behaving as if that conversation had never happened. But deep inside, she wondered if she should tell him what was troubling her.

"What did you name the stars?" Chance asked his

mother, pulling Sophie back into the night's festivities and giving her something else to think about.

"We called some of them tic-tac-toe because they were in the shapes of *X*s and *O*s," Libby replied.

Matt piped up and said, "I thought we called them hugs and kisses." He reached for his fiancée's hand and gave it a light squeeze.

She flashed her dimples at him. "Maybe it was a bit of both." She turned her attention back to her son. "Do you want to name some of them now?"

"Heck, yeah." He wiggled in the straw. "Tommy and Sophie can help me. Come on, guys. Let's give 'em better names than my mom and Matt did. Tic-tac-toe is okay. But hugs and kisses… That's kind of stupid."

Tommy laughed. "You won't think it's stupid when you're older. But let's give it a go and see what we can do." He gazed up at the sky. "I've never seen this many stars until I came here, and I've been all over the world."

Chance scooted closer to him. "Where's your most favorite place you've ever been?"

"Honestly, I don't know. I've enjoyed them all. But there is one place I'd like to go that I've never been."

"Where's that?" the boy excitedly asked.

Tommy smiled. "Neverland. Or Never Land or whatever you want to call it."

Chance's eyes went big and round. "Where Peter Pan and Captain Hook and all of them are?"

Tommy nodded. "Sophie looked like Peter Pan

when she was little. She had pixie hair like his. And she was tough and scrappy and boyish." He winked at her. "Sometimes I even used to call her Pan, and she'd get mad and throw sticks at me, saying that I was more like him because of how boastful I was." He softened his voice. "We've both grown up since then, but Neverland still reminds me of her."

While Sophie's heart skipped a foolishly dreamy beat, Chance roamed his curious gaze over her. Was he trying to picture her the way she'd just been described?

The child turned back to Tommy and said, "We should name the stars after the people in Peter Pan."

"Sure." Tommy leaned against the back of the wagon, his knees bent in front of him. "That'll be fun. But from here, they all pretty much look like Tinker Bell."

The six-year-old appeared to contemplate that and come to a conclusion. "Then that's who all of them can be, except the ones we give other names to." He gazed up at the night sky, an earnest expression on his little face. "That bunch over there can be Captain Hook and his crew. And that one by itself can be the alligator who ate off Hook's hand."

Tommy chuckled. "Well, that sounds gnarly."

Sophie meant to laugh, too. But she remained quiet, immersed in watching Tommy and Chance. She glanced over at Matt and Libby. They were watching the scene unfold, too.

Tommy pointed upward. "Should that group at the very top be Peter Pan and the Lost Boys?"

Chance followed his line of sight. A second later, he looked at Sophie. "If that's okay with her, then it's okay with me."

She smiled, touched that he was taking her Pan persona so seriously. "It's totally fine with me. I think Peter and his friends would like that spot."

The boy returned her smile and finished his task by naming a star after Wendy. But hers wasn't quite as bright. According to his youthful wisdom, Wendy was just a normal girl who was going to grow old. Someday her star would burn out.

To keep from going sad, Sophie thought about how many Tinker Bell stars were twinkling down on them and wondered if she should make a wish. Or maybe she should just get her head out of the sky and work on staying grounded.

The wagon bumped along, with Sophie trying not to frown.

Once they arrived at the campsite, Matt and Tommy helped the ranch attendants build the fires, and Sophie and Libby unpacked the supplies.

Later, as they sat at their campfire eating s'mores, Chance made a sticky mess, gobbling up the treats and wiping his hands on his pants. He ignored the packages of wet wipes that had been provided. He even dropped one into the dirt.

After Libby picked up the packet and dusted it off, Matt told a nice story. He revealed that he and

Libby had gotten engaged on National S'mores Day and would be getting married on that same day next summer.

Sophie commented on how "sweet" their wedding was going to be, and everyone else laughed. But she wasn't laughing herself. As she admired the other couple with their marshmallow-and-chocolate-smeared child tucked between them, she fretted about her feelings for Tommy.

He leaned over and whispered, "You okay?"

"I'm fine." Hating that she'd gotten caught with a less-than-happy expression, she plastered a smile on her lips. But maybe once they got home, she would give up the fight and tell him what was wrong, and admit how deeply afraid she was of loving him.

Eleven

The Texas weekend ended, and on Monday morning Sophie was at work, debating what to do about Tommy. Should she talk to him tonight after dinner? Should she tell him about her struggle?

Yes, she thought, she should. If she didn't, her feelings were going to eat her alive. She wished she could leave the office early and just get it over with. She could feign morning sickness, she supposed. So far, she wasn't having any of those symptoms. But she hated to lie to Barbara and pretend to be ill when she was feeling fine. Or as fine as an anxiety-ridden pregnant woman could be.

Hours later while Sophie was immersed in paperwork, her cell phone rang. She saw Tommy's name on the screen and answered it.

"Soph?" he said right away. "I need to talk to you."

She noticed that he sounded upset. "Is everything all right?"

"No, it's not. Something happened, but I don't want to get into it over the phone."

She panicked. "Is someone hurt?"

"It's nothing like that. It's just…" He hesitated, blowing a raspy breath into the receiver. "I need for you to come home so we can discuss it in person."

"Should I do that right now?" The urgency in his tone worried her, and she was already having issues of her own. This certainly wasn't helping her anxiety. Whatever was wrong in Tommy's world sounded serious.

"Yes, but don't tell Barbara you're leaving because I'm freaking out. This is personal, and I don't want anyone to know besides you. Brandon knows, but he's my lawyer, so I had to tell him."

Sophie couldn't begin to guess what was going on, especially since Tommy had involved Brandon. "Maybe I can tell Barbara that I'm not feeling well. That I have morning sickness or something." It was the excuse she'd considered earlier.

"Sure, that will work. In fact, you can tell her that I called to check up on you, and you told me that you were sick. So I insisted that you come home and rest."

Sophie wished that she actually was returning to the mansion to relax. Tommy's unease was making her tense. "I'll be there as soon as I can."

"Okay. Thanks." He paused. "And I'm sorry, Soph. I'm so sorry."

Her heart punched against her ribs. Was he apologizing for making her rush home? Or was it the news itself that required an apology?

They ended the call, and she smoothed her dress, trying to compose herself. She left her office and headed down the hall, to Barbara's. The door was partially open. She poked in her head, but she knocked, too.

Barbara glanced up from her computer and waved Sophie inside. At forty-six, she was a hardworking Southern gal who wore her dyed red hair expertly coiffed. She had a truck-driver husband and three teenage sons who drove her batty. Tommy sometimes overwhelmed her, too. But he had that effect on the people who worked for him; Sophie was no exception.

Between her fear of falling in love with him and whatever problems he was currently facing, she was getting more nervous by the minute.

She approached the other woman's desk and said, "I'm not feeling well." She went into her morning-sickness spiel, also repeating what Tommy told her to say.

"Oh, sugar, don't worry about needing to go home. I was as sick and surly as an old hound dog with my kids. Sipping cola syrup used to help. Keeping crackers and pretzels beside my bed and at my desk was a lifesaver, too. I heard that some women sniff lemons to alleviate their symptoms. It's supposed to be an aromatherapy thing." The redhead sighed. "But if it gets really bad, you can get a prescription for an antiemetic drug."

Sophie had already discussed morning-sickness remedies with her doctor, but she appreciated Barbara's input. "I'll check back with you tomorrow. I just need to get off my feet today." By now, her story wasn't so much of a lie. She was getting weary. But whether it was the baby or a reaction to the stress, she couldn't say.

Barbara wished her well, and Sophie left the office and climbed into her truck. She rolled down the windows, taking refuge in the cool November air.

By the time she got to the mansion, she'd already listened to a slew of songs on her playlist. None of them were Tommy's. As nervous as she was, she couldn't handle his music today.

She entered the property through the main gate and drove around back. She didn't want to risk seeing Dottie or Chef Bryan or anyone else. Instead, she took the poolside steps that led directly to Tommy's suite.

He was in his bedroom, trapped in a state of dishevelment. He'd made a mess out of his hair—he'd obviously tugged his hands through it—and he'd rubbed his forehead raw, the friction making his skin turn red. He was rubbing it now, even pressing his fingers against his eyes.

"You look awful, Tommy."

"I'm so scared, Soph." He came toward her. "And I'm worried about how this is going to impact you."

"Just tell me what it is." She needed for him to come clean. "Just say it."

"I just found out that Kara's baby could be mine, after all."

She felt the color drain from her face. "What?"

"The lab that did the paternity test called today and said there might've been a mix-up in the results and that I might actually be the father instead of the other man."

"Oh, my God." Sophie sat on the edge of the bed. She could barely think straight. "How is it even possible to mix up a test like that?"

"They think the labels on the vials of blood might've gotten switched. They just discovered that a disgruntled employee was deliberately tampering with stuff, and it's possible that our samples were compromised by this person. We won't know until we retake the test."

"Then that's what you'll have to do." She rocked forward, clutching her stomach. No way was she going to allow herself to love Tommy. Or tell him that she'd been struggling with it. She was already in deeper than she should be. "Did you talk to Kara?"

He nodded. "I called her, and she's freaking out, too. She's afraid that if the baby is mine, she'll lose the other man."

"She's in love with him?" Sophie had wondered about that all along.

Tommy nodded again. "She told me that his name

is Dan, and she met him a few days after she was with me. She was on the rebound from her ex, and that's why she hooked up with me. But she said it was different with Dan. That she developed a true closeness with him, an immediate bond."

"It's too bad that she didn't meet Dan before she had that one-night stand with you."

"That's what she said. She hadn't meant to be with two guys in the same week, but she liked Dan so much, she slept with him, too. She used protection with both of us. But obviously it failed with at least one of us." Tommy squeezed his eyes shut for a second. "She and Dan started a relationship, but she didn't tell him about me, not until she found out she was pregnant."

Sophie contemplated Kara's plight. At that point, she could have pretended the baby was Dan's and left Tommy out of it. Of course, Sophie wouldn't have done that, either. Not with something as important as the paternity of a child.

Tommy cleared his throat. "This nearly destroyed them the first time, waiting to see whose kid it was. And now they're going through it again. But it's worse this time, all these months later. Dan is having a breakdown over it. They both are."

Sophie kept her arms around her stomach, holding on to her baby. "I can only imagine the toll it's taking on their relationship."

"Kara told me that it's a boy. She had an ultrasound a little while ago. Dan was excited about having a son, and now it might not even be his." Tommy rubbed his forehead, making the red spot redder. "I'm scared out of my mind, but I can't just walk away if the kid is mine. I'd have to try to be his father, to be involved in his life, somehow." He sat beside her. "And then there's your baby. I think I should be a father to him or her, too."

She flinched. At first he didn't want any children and now he was willing to claim both of them? "I understand that you're trying to do the right thing by taking responsibility for Kara's son, but that doesn't have anything to do with me."

"You're my closest friend, Soph. I should be the father to your baby, as much as I should be to hers."

"No, you shouldn't." She didn't want him to parent her child, not out of guilt or duty or obligation. If he loved her, then maybe it would be different. But he wasn't talking love. He was talking friendship. "You're the donor. That's what we agreed on. That's the contract we both signed."

"I'd try to be a good dad. I promise I would."

He sounded beautifully sincere. But that only made her feel worse. "That's not how this is supposed to work." She couldn't let him change the rules, not at the expense of how painful it was for her. "We need to keep things as they are." *No,* she thought, *not as they are*. Things needed to return to normal. "Actually, I should go home. I can't keep staying here. I can't keep doing this." She already wanted to curl into a ball and cry.

He frowned. "Do you regret us being lovers?"

She regretted the holes that he'd poked into her heart, but she didn't have the courage to say that. "It's not going to help either of us to lament what we should or shouldn't have done. We just need to move past it."

"I'm going to miss you not living here." He touched her arm briefly, cautiously. "I'll miss you so much."

She was tortured over leaving, too. But it couldn't be helped. "Our affair was always supposed to end."

"I know, but this seems like an awful way to let go."

It was beyond awful, she thought, especially with her fears of loving him. "I'm going to start packing now."

"I have to see my doctor. I promised Kara that I would have my blood drawn right away, so they can send it to the lab that finalizes the results. But I can help you move your stuff over later."

"I'd prefer that someone from your staff did it. But thank you for the offer." She studied his forlorn expression, wishing that she could make him feel better. But she couldn't even do that for herself. "Did you tell Kara about us? That I'm pregnant and you're the donor?"

He shook his head. "I would never do that without your consent. Telling her wouldn't have changed anything, anyway. She would still be dealing with her own problems."

Sophie felt bad for Kara and how she might lose the man she loved if the results didn't go in his favor. But on the other hand, should it really matter? "Do you think Dan loves Kara as much as she loves him?"

Tommy shrugged. "I don't know. I guess so."

"Well, if he does, then he should accept her and the child. Even if the baby doesn't turn out to be his, he can still stay with Kara and help her raise it. And you can still be its father, too."

"I wish you'd reconsider my role in Peanut's life."

His nickname for the baby made her hurt even more. "Your role is the same as it's always been." She stood and moved away from the bed. "I'm sorry, but I really need to go home."

He came to his feet, too. "When will I get to see you again?"

"You can call me or come by when you get the test results." She owed him that much.

"It normally takes about a week, but they're supposed to put a rush on it. Brandon said we could sue the lab for the duress this has caused, but I don't want to create more havoc."

"Try to relax until you hear something." She didn't know what else to say to him.

"You need to take care of yourself, too."

"I'll be okay." She headed for the closet to get her suitcases.

When she glanced back at Tommy, she noticed that he was watching her, with a painful goodbye in his eyes.

The following day, Sophie got morning sickness for real. At first it was just a bout of queasiness. So she nibbled on crackers. But that didn't work. So she sniffed a lemon, which didn't help, either. As the nausea progressed, she ran to the toilet, vomiting to the point of exhaustion.

Later, after her stomach settled, she brewed a cup of chamomile tea and called Barbara, letting her know that she wasn't coming into the office today. Between being ill this morning and yesterday's news, she was just too worn-out.

To keep from going hungry, she made some dry toast and ate it slowly. So far, so good. She wasn't having afternoon sickness, too.

She went into the living room and sat on the couch. God help her, but she missed Tommy. She even wondered if she should agree to let him be the father to her child.

No, she thought. Her life was already too entwined with his. She couldn't handle a deeper connection to him, not if it meant battling her heart for control. Besides, how long would it be before Tommy started hanging out with groupies again? Before he went back to his old lifestyle? She didn't want to be witness to that.

So maybe she should quit working for him and move out of Nashville. She could relocate to Los Angeles. There were plenty of music-related jobs there.

Tommy could come to LA and visit now and then, she told herself. He could still be a friend.

A faraway friend. A man in the distance.

But wasn't that better than staying here and fighting her feelings for him? He would still be the donor.

Her son or daughter would still be told who he was. He just wouldn't be living nearby. Then again, with the way he traveled, he wouldn't be around Nashville much, anyway.

She glanced over at her dogs, where they were curled up near the fireplace. Hokey and Pokey seemed depressed now that they were home. They missed Tommy as much as she did, especially with the way he spoiled them. Unfortunately, she didn't know how to cheer them up. She could barely cope with her own turmoil.

The doorbell rang, chiming noisily. The dogs barked and ran to the door, eager to discover who it was. Sophie assumed it was a ranch hand from Tommy's stables bringing her horses back.

But she was wrong. It was Tommy himself. Except that the horses weren't with him. There was no trailer attached to his truck.

"May I come in?" he asked, as he knelt to pet the pooches. They danced happily at his feet.

"Why don't I come out there?" She didn't want to be cooped up in the house with him. Now that he was here, she decided that she needed as much fresh air as she could get.

They sat side by side on the porch steps, and she hurriedly asked, "Did you get word from the lab already? I didn't know it would be this soon."

"There's no news yet."

"Are they going to call you when the results are in?"

"No. They'll be sending them, like they did last time. That's the standard procedure." He angled his body a bit more toward hers. "But that isn't the reason I stopped by."

Her pulse skittered. "Then what is it?"

"I called Kara today and asked for Dan's number. I wanted to talk to him about what you said."

Sophie started. "About his feelings for Kara?"

"Not in so many words, but yeah. I just told him that no matter whose baby it is, he can still be part of its life if he wants to be with Kara. I also told him that I hope things work out for them."

"How did he react to what you said?" she asked, trying to keep her voice from betraying her. She hadn't expected him to take her views about the other couple so deeply.

"He seemed to appreciate it. But I don't know if it helped. He really wants the kid to be his." He leaned forward. "And do you know what I want?" He answered his own question. "For you to agree to let me be the father of your baby."

"I just think it's better if you remain the donor," she said. "I'm probably going to be moving. I was thinking of going to LA."

"What?" He looked as if he'd just stopped breathing.

"I need a change, to start over with the baby."

"I knew something was wrong in Texas. Dammit, I knew I was going to lose you. That our friendship might be ending." His voice went shaky. "I never meant for what I did with Kara to affect you, and I'm so sorry for the stress it caused. But why did you start pulling away from me when we were in Texas? What's going on, Soph? It can't just be this added problem with Kara. Not when I noticed it before."

She couldn't say it. She just couldn't admit that she was afraid of loving him. Or how badly she wished that he would love her, too, in a fully committed way. Tommy had been loyal to her during their affair, but that didn't mean he'd morphed into a one-woman kind of man. "We'll still be friends and you can still visit me. Besides, you'll be back on the road before you know it, living the life you love."

"I can't believe that you want to leave this area. Nashville is where you were raised. This is your home, the place where you've always belonged."

"I can belong somewhere else." She had to find a way to do that. Desperate to escape the confusion she saw on his face, she said, "I hope you don't mind, but I want to go inside and rest. I got sick this morning, and I'm beat."

He searched her gaze. "Can I do anything to help?"

He could love her, she thought. "No, there's nothing. But you can still contact me when you get the paternity results."

He helped her to her feet. "I don't want you to move away."

"I can't talk about this right now." She took her hand away from his. "I need to lie down."

And try to keep herself from crying.

Tommy paced Brandon's office, immersed in panic and fear. Two days had passed since he'd seen Sophie, and all he'd done was obsess about losing her. He couldn't stand the thought of her going to LA and raising the baby there.

As for the other baby, he still didn't know if it was his. The results were supposed to arrive by special delivery in tomorrow's mail. But at the moment, that seemed like light-years away. Everything did.

"You need to chill out," Brandon said.

Tommy scowled at him. Chill out? Was he kidding? "I talked to Matt yesterday and told him what was going on."

"About Sophie wanting to move or about Kara's baby?"

"About both. I thought he would be a good authority on women and children and all of that. But he sounded a little cautious when I mentioned Sophie."

"Cautious how?"

"I don't know, exactly. There was just something in his voice. But then I figured he was probably just uncomfortable about being dragged into it. The only advice he gave me was to be patient with Sophie." But how could Tommy be patient if she left the area? He wouldn't even be seeing her. "I'm not saying that this new problem with Kara isn't an issue, but something was already going on with Sophie before that happened. And you know what makes it worse? That Dad was right. He kept saying that my baby arrangement with Sophie was going to create problems."

"You didn't tell Dad about what's going on now, did you?"

"Hell, no. It was hard enough to tell you and Matt. I don't want Dad rubbing my problems in my face."

Brandon left his chair and came around to the other side of the desk. "I should have advised you the way Dad did. I should have told you to think twice before signing the donor contract. But honestly, I never expected you to change your mind and want to be a father. I never figured Sophie for wanting to skip town, either. With how tight your friendship has always been, it seemed like a solid arrangement to me. But either way, I'm proud of you, brother."

Tommy blinked at him. "You are? Why?"

"For trying to do right by both babies. And for being respectful of Dan and Kara's relationship."

"I just wish Sophie wasn't shutting me out. She started pulling away once she got pregnant, and she seemed even more preoccupied while we were in Texas. I mentioned it to her while we were there, but it didn't make a difference. I understand that things went awry after we got back, and this situation with Kara is probably pushing her over the edge now." He couldn't deny his part in that. "I feel awful that something from my past is creating stress and anxiety for her. Just so damn awful." Sophie was the last person in the world he ever wanted to hurt. "But I still think there's more going on with her. Something she isn't telling me. She says we'll still be friends, but it doesn't feel that way to me."

Brandon leaned against his desk. "Maybe something happened in Texas that you're not aware of, and that's why Matt sounded so cautious. He might actually know what it is."

Tommy's pulse jumped. "I need to talk to him again."

His brother went into lawyer mode. "We can call him, right now, both of us together. Better yet, let's get him on Skype. I think he'll be more likely to tell us what's going on if we can see him face-to-face."

"And you can grill him?" Tommy was willing to do anything at this point.

They arranged a video chat for an hour later. When Matt appeared on the computer screen, he looked dusty, as if he'd been out riding or working the ranch.

Brandon jumped right in and ambushed him, and soon Matt was squirming under fire. He even pulled his hat lower, shielding his eyes as if that might help.

"It's not my place to talk about it," Matt said.

"Talk about what?" the attorney pressed.

"About what Sophie told Libby. Hell, Libby probably shouldn't have even repeated it to me."

"I understand that you're trying to protect Sophie's privacy and not get into trouble with your own woman over it." Brandon shoved Tommy toward the monitor. "But look at this guy. If you don't tell him what's going on, he's going to lose his mind."

Matt lifted the brim of his hat and stared at Tommy. After a beat of silence he said, "You need to ask Sophie what's going on. She should be the one to tell you."

Tommy replied, "I've been asking her what's wrong, and all she does is pull further away from me. Please, just tell me what she told Libby."

Matt made a pained expression. "Okay, but if this comes back to bite me in the ass, I'm holding you responsible."

"Fine. I'll take the heat." He would take anything anyone threw his way.

His Texas half brother blew out a ragged breath. "All right. Here it is. She's afraid of her feelings."

"Her feelings about what?" Tommy was as confused as ever.

"About you."

Tommy still wasn't getting it. "About me being the donor or the dad or what?"

Matt shook his head. Clearly, he thought Tommy was being dense. Did Brandon think so, too? Sure enough, he was shaking his head, as well.

"What am I missing?" Tommy asked.

Finally Matt said, "She's afraid of falling in love with you." He gently added, "Is that plain enough? Does that explain it?"

Yes? No? God help him. Tommy dropped onto a

chair. He shouldn't have pursued this. He shouldn't have asked Matt to tell him. Because now that he knew, he was afraid, too.

So damn scared of what it all meant.

Twelve

Tommy went home, changed into his swim trunks and dived into the pool. The winter air was cool, and the water was warm.

He couldn't stop thinking about love and what it meant. He had no idea what being in love felt like. But he knew that it could be good or bad, blissful or painful. He'd seen it happen to enough people, where they either flourished from it or curled up and died. He'd been an observer, watching from the sidelines, and now he was drowning in Sophie's fear of it, triggering fears of his own.

He swam over to the second waterfall, submerged himself beneath it and headed for his underground lair.

Once he entered the apartment, he pushed his hair

out of his eyes and grabbed a towel. Images of Sophie were playing in his mind from the night of the masquerade, when he'd brought her here. Now on this moonlit evening he was alone, sulking like the phantom that inspired the mask he'd worn.

Everything reminded him of Sophie: his house, his music, his family, his childhood. She'd been a part of nearly every aspect of his life. If she left town, he didn't know what he was going to do without her.

He went to the fridge and grabbed a sparkling water, uncapped the bottle and took a bubbly swig.

Sophie was obviously hurting over him. He was hurting over her, too. He ached inside, his emotions twisting him in two.

He kept saying that he was going to write an album about his affair with her. But the songs would only be mournful ballads. Because, really, who was he trying to kid by saying that he didn't know what being in love felt like?

Sophie had always been the number one person in his life, and he could barely function without her.

He'd been with scores of other women over the years, but he'd never gotten attached to any of them. With Sophie, the two of them had been joined at the hip. At the heart. At the soul.

What they shared was more than physical, and the equation added up to love. Tommy loved her, pure and simple.

No, he thought. There was nothing pure or simple about it. If he went to her this very instant, offering to make a commitment, to marry her and raise their child together, he would also be asking her to accept the results of the paternity test, regardless of the outcome.

If Kara's baby belonged to Tommy, there was no denying that the press would chastise him for having two kids with two different women. And if Sophie chose to stay with him, she would get dragged through the mud, too. The internet trolls would criticize her at every turn. It wouldn't be easy on the kids, either. He knew from experience what having a famous father was like. Yet in spite of that, Tommy had sought fame and fortune, too.

He frowned at the water bottle in his hand. He understood why Sophie was fighting her feelings for him. Regardless of how deep their attraction was, he'd never had the qualities she'd yearned for in a man. She'd refused to date him in the past because he didn't know how to settle down. Because he was too restless, too wild, with too many women around.

Only things were different now. He loved Sophie, and he didn't want anyone except her. She was it for him, the person he wanted to spend the rest of his life with.

But with how precarious everything else was, how was it going to work between them? Not just with the Kara situation, but with his job, too. How would Sophie cope with him going back out on the road? Would she expect him to alter his career and stay home with her?

Tommy had a lot to think about, so many jumbled things tormenting his mind and making a mess out of his heart.

On Thursday afternoon, Sophie got a text from Tommy asking if she would come to his house. He'd received the paternity-test results, but he didn't want to open the envelope unless she was with him. She assumed he was too nervous to do it alone, so she agreed to meet him in his garden. For her, it was a neutral location. She couldn't bear to return to his suite. Being in the vicinity of his bedroom would only make her ache more than she already did. She missed cuddling in his arms at night. She missed him during the day, too. She just plain missed him.

What choice did she have, except to leave Nashville? She needed to find a way to survive without being consumed by him, without his mansion being nearby, without everything that reminded her of him.

She'd taken the week off from work, but she hadn't given her notice yet. She hadn't put her house on the market yet, either. But as soon as this meeting with Tommy was over, she would be doing both of those things.

Sophie cut across the lawn and took the garden path. She passed the tiger statue and headed to the koi pond, where Tommy was supposed to be waiting for her.

She spotted him soon enough—tall and long and lean in his slim-fitting jeans and black vintage Western shirt. Sometimes he favored those old styles. This one had red-rose embroidery and white piping. She was familiar with the design. She'd given it to him on his last birthday, but she hadn't expected him to be wearing it today.

He turned in Sophie's direction, and her heart skipped anxious beats. He was holding the unopened envelope, the yet-unknown paternity results, in his hand.

"Hi, Soph," he said, once they were close enough to speak.

She sucked in her breath and repeated his greeting. "Hi."

They sat beside each other on an ornate iron bench. When he folded the envelope and tucked it into his shirt pocket, she got confused.

She said, "I thought you were going to open that once I got here."

"I don't want to know the results just yet. First I want to talk to you about something." His leg was jittering, bouncing up and down.

She considered putting her hand on his knee to help calm him, but she didn't. She was too antsy herself. "If I was in your position, I would want to know right away."

"I'm prepared for either outcome. But what I'm not prepared for is losing you."

Her pulse went haywire, was now even jumpier than his leg. "What do you mean?"

"I've been thinking a lot about the pain I've been

in since you moved out. And now you're talking about leaving Nashville. With everything going on, I keep coming back to that. I've never felt pain like this before."

"I know that it probably seems cowardly for me to run away. But I can't just hang around here and be your friend. It hurts too much, Tommy."

"But that's what I'm saying. I can't live without you, and I finally understand what that means. I love you, and I want us to have a life together, you and me and our baby. But I'm worried about how it'll affect you if the other child is mine, about how the press will treat the situation and the emotional impact it will have on you. There are other things to consider, too, like me going back out on the road. I came up with a partial solution to that, but it still might not be right for you."

Sophie was still reeling from his initial admission, let alone having the ability to focus on the rest of it. "You love me? Since when?"

"Since the beginning, but I didn't know it, not until I was losing you. I just took it for granted that you'd always be there for me, and I was wrong to expect that from you. You deserve better than someone like me."

"So what are you saying? That you want us to be together, but you don't think it'll work?"

"I just don't want to make life harder for you. I want to be the man who makes you happy, not the guy who creates agony and stress."

"It matters that you love me." It mattered more than she could say. She *never, ever* thought she would hear those words from him.

"Is there a chance you feel the same way, too?"

She nodded, barely able to contain her emotion. "Yes. My God, yes! But I'm still scared of the things you said. Are you sure that you want to be with me, Tommy? It's not just about the situation with Kara and with our baby?"

"I'm positive about how I feel. But that doesn't change the hardship that us being together might cause you."

The look in his eyes was so deep and sincere, she wanted to cry. "No one said love was supposed to be easy."

"I know, but I'm just about the worst catch there is. Who in their right mind would want me as a husband?"

Her heart leaped to her throat. "Is marriage on the table?"

"It is, if you want it to be. But you'd have to be sure, more certain than you've ever been about anything in your life."

In spite of the anxiety still swirling around them, she actually laughed. "That's the most troubling proposal I've ever heard."

He laughed, too. "I know. I'm sorry. But I've been up all night stressing about this." His expression turned serious. "I want to fight for you—I want to convince you that I'm the man of your dreams. But how can I be your dream man if I've never been the type of guy you wanted?"

"I always wanted you. I just didn't want to share you with a zillion other women."

"There's never going to be anyone ever again. It's just you, Soph. It'll always be just you from now on." He looked longingly at her. "Commitment used to scare me, but it feels right with you. Do you believe me? Do you trust me?"

"Yes." He wouldn't have asked her to marry him if he didn't mean it. Tommy knew better than to toy with commitment, especially with how disloyal his father had been to his mother. "I trust you."

"But what about Kara's baby?" He took the envelope out of his pocket. "If this child is mine, it's going to affect you, too. The media will tear me apart for having two kids with two different women, and people will slam you for being with me."

She refused to back down. "I'll just have to learn to handle what they dish out."

"It'll be tough on the kids, too."

She put her hand on her tummy. "I wouldn't allow either baby to be hurt. Kara's son would be mine as much as he would be yours. And I would hope that Dan would be protective of both babies, too, regardless of who fathered them."

He gazed at her as if she was the most amazing person on earth. "You really mean all of that, don't you?"

"Yes, I do." She didn't want to run away from

him anymore. She wanted to stay and fight for the love between them. She took the envelope from him, but she didn't open it. She tucked it into her pocket, giving them time to finish their conversation. "Now first tell me about the partial solution you've come up with to you going back out on the road."

He smiled softly, a bit shakily, and was still giving her an awed look. "I was thinking that I could take the reality-show deal so I could stay here with you and our baby for the next few years. Then when it's time for the *Music Mentors* tour, I was hoping that you and Peanut could travel with me. I know you never wanted to haul a kid around on the road, but touring is part of my job. And if we did it as a family, maybe it would be a nice adventure."

"That sounds like a beautiful compromise." She recognized the sacrifices they would both be making. But Sophie wanted nothing more than for her and Tommy and their child to be a family. She reached into her pocket and removed the envelope. "Should I open this? Or do you want to do it?"

"You can do it."

She tore open the seal and removed the results. She glanced at the paper and revealed what it said. "You're not the father, Tommy."

He only stared at her for a second. "I'm not?" He took the paper from her and read it himself.

Then he reached for her, and they held each other, warm and tight.

His mouth sought hers, and they kissed, the two of

them wrapped in love and commitment. And friendship, she thought.

Tommy was still her oldest and dearest friend, only now he was going to be her husband, too.

Tommy took Sophie's hand and led her to the mansion. Where she belonged, he thought, where they could be together.

They ascended the private staircase that led to his suite. He was so anxious for the future to unfold that he wanted to start planning their wedding right away. But first they needed to get properly engaged.

Once they were inside his room, he said, "I have something to give you." He went to his nightstand and opened the drawer. He removed the ring he'd bought her from its case and turned to face her. He hadn't brought it outside with him because he'd been afraid to presume that she would marry him. So he'd kept it here, shrouded in hope.

Her eyes went wide, and he went down on bended knee. "I love you, Sophia Marie Cardinale, and I'm going to do everything in my power to be the best husband and father I can be." He released the breath he'd been holding. Making it official, he asked, "Will you marry me?"

Her eyes glistened with tears. "Yes, I absolutely will."

He slid the five-carat solitaire onto her finger and came to his feet. "When I told my jeweler that I wanted a diamond that shined as bright as a star, he said that the ancient Romans considered diamonds to be pieces of stars that had fallen to earth. So that's what this is. A piece of one of the stars we named in Texas."

"It's incredible." She gazed at the ring. "I can't wait to marry you. My father really liked you, Tommy. I think my mother would have, too. Dad always told me what a romantic she was."

"I wish I could have met her. That she could have lived to be part of your life, and mine, too. She's going to be looking down on you on our wedding day. Both of your parents will be there."

"Is it okay with you if I ask your dad to walk me down the aisle? I'd like for him to fill in for my father."

"He'll be thrilled, I'm sure. My mom will be jumping for joy that we're getting married, too."

"We'll have to figure out a way for her to be part of the ceremony, as well. We can't leave her out of it."

"Should we do it here at the mansion? As soon as we can? I don't want to wait or have a long engagement."

"Me, neither. How about a March wedding? That's only four months away and should be just in time for my first ultrasound."

"That works for me. It'll be a whirlwind, but we can pull it off." Tommy had the money and the resources to make it happen in a quick and grand way. "Brandon can be my best man, and Matt can be one of my ushers."

She smiled. "I'll include Libby as one of my bridesmaids. And Chance can be our ring bearer. I'm not sure about the flower girl. Maybe one of Mack and Jean's daughters."

He put his hand on her tummy. "I'm starting to get the feeling that Peanut will be a girl."

"Really? Why?"

"I don't know. Daddy intuition, I guess." He paused. "I want this to be a family-style wedding. I can enlist a nanny service to help with everyone's kids. At some point, we're going to need our own nanny, too, especially when we're on the road. It wouldn't hurt to have an extra set of hands."

She slipped her arms around his waist. "That sounds good to me. I'm just excited to become your wife."

"The next four months are going to be crazy, with the CMAs, Christmas, New Year's and our wedding."

"I almost forgot about the CMAs."

"They changed the time slot, scheduling them a little later this year. I'm not nominated this time, but they asked me to be a presenter."

"Oh, poor boy." She teased him. "You've won Record of the Year and Entertainer of the Year for the past two years. It's time to give someone else a chance."

"Yeah, well, when I produce an album with songs about you and our baby, I'll be winning all sorts of future awards for it. Yesterday I worried about how downhearted my new songs were going to be. But today, I know that they're going to be my best ever."

She laughed. "There you go, boasting as usual. Call me crazy, but I love that side of you."

He grinned. "I just pretend to be conceited, remember? But I'm glad you love my ego as much as the rest of me." He swept her off her feet and carried her to bed. He loved everything about her, this perfect woman who'd agreed to be his wife.

Tommy's hands on Sophie's body felt magnificent. So warm, she thought. So passionate. He removed her clothes, touching her in places that made her sigh and arch and purr.

Whatever made her think that she could live without him? She was still aching from the need to be close to him, and he was right there. Tommy. *Her* Tommy. He belonged to her now, just as she belonged to him.

He went down on her, lifting her hips and raising her bottom in the air. She gripped his shoulders as he did deliciously wicked things with his tongue. Soft and silky heat, she thought, and wild, wild wetness.

The diamond on her finger shimmered in the light. He'd captured a piece of a star and given it to her. He was a star, too, she thought. A superstar who entertained millions of people with his music, and she was his biggest admirer.

He gazed up at her, his hazel eyes changing colors.

Sophie was trying to hold on, to make this moment last, but she was already spiraling toward an orgasm.

He smiled like a mischievous schoolboy and pushed her over the edge, making her come.

Shaking and shuddering, she closed her eyes and tugged on his hair, the short, stylishly messy strands slipping through her fingers.

While the room seemed to spin, she felt him shift his weight. She opened her eyes and saw that he'd climbed on top of her, his face temptingly close to hers.

She reached for him, and they rolled over the bed, kissing and caressing and making hungry sounds. She pulled open the snaps on his shirt and bared his chest. She shoved her hands down his jeans, too, giving him an even bigger hard-on than he already had.

"Damn," he said. "What you do to me."

"Likewise." Her skin was tingling from her orgasm, her body still damp from where he used his tongue. "I want you inside me now."

"Yes, ma'am." He exaggerated his country charm and dragged his jeans past his hips.

He didn't take them all the way off, but she didn't mind. It seemed hotter this way, the desperation between them turning her on. He thrust into her, and she dug her nails into the part of his ass that was exposed.

He moved inside her, the friction from his pants abrading her bare legs. She curled her toes and keened out a moan. He kept going, deeper and deeper, every thrust more thrilling than the last. Flesh melded with flesh, twirling and spinning into a chasm of lust.

And love, Sophie thought. So much love.

The sex was ragged, but the commitment between them was gentle. They took a moment to savor it.

"Together," she whispered.

"Always," he whispered back, thrusting warm and deep.

She kissed him, and they tumbled over the bed again, locked in intensity. They messed up the covers, knocking pillows onto the floor. His body tensed, his abs rippled.

She thrashed beneath him, and he tossed back his head and spilled into her. She came, too, his climax jump-starting hers.

In the afterglow, he held her. She didn't know how much time passed, but the room was still brightly lit and immersed in daylight. Eventually, their breathing slowed and the sheen of sweat on their bodies evaporated. When they separated, they retrieved the fallen pillows and rested their heads on them.

"If I had already proposed to you, I would ask you to marry me all over again," he finally said.

"And I would say yes again." She would marry him a million times.

He shifted onto his elbow. "I can't believe we almost lost each other."

"I'm so glad we didn't." She turned to look at him. "Are we still going to tell our donor story in your dad's biography?"

"Sure. Why not? Only now it'll be a story about friends who made a baby and fell in love." He skimmed a hand down her stomach. "Are you going to let me attend your doctor visits now that we're a couple?"

"Yes, of course, and I'm not going to care who sees us or Tweets about it. If I'm going to be your wife, then I'm going to have to get friendlier with your fans. I might have to start Tweeting more myself. I can even change my Twitter handle to Mrs. Tommy Talbot."

"You'll be famous, too." He kept touching her tummy, his fingertips light and gentle. "Speaking of which, you'll have to get used to having your own bodyguard. And walking red carpets." He circled her navel. "Will you go to the CMAs with me?"

"I'd be honored." She smiled. "It'll be our first date without wearing masks."

He smiled, as well. "Can I announce our engagement to the press at the after-parties?"

"You most certainly can." She didn't want to keep anything hidden anymore, not after what they'd just been through. "You can tell them you're going to be a daddy, too."

"Really?" He searched her gaze. "You don't want to wait until the first trimester is over?"

"I don't want to wait for anything." She wanted the world to know that she and Tommy were going to be parents. "I'm not worried about jinxing it anymore, not with as happy as I am."

"Who knew we could be this kind of happy?" He

made a perplexed expression. "I wonder if Brandon will ever find anyone."

She raised her eyebrows. "You're concerned about your brother's bachelorhood?" First he was trying to help Kara and Dan stay together, and now he was thinking about Brandon. Sophie couldn't help but be amused. Tommy the matchmaker. "I wouldn't mess with your brother's love life if I were you. I don't think he would appreciate that."

"I'm not going to say anything to him about it. But now that I have you, and Matt has Libby, he's going to be the odd man out."

"If he's meant to find someone, he will."

"Yeah. You're right. If there's a woman out there for him, he'll drive her as crazy as I drove you."

Sophie moistened her lips. "You Talbot men are a dangerous breed." She glanced down. He'd pulled up his jeans, but he hadn't zipped them all the way. She ran her hand along the denim. "I'm going to want you again."

He climbed on top of her. "That can be arranged."

They kissed, and he rubbed against her, showing her that he wanted her again, too. Hot and dreamy, she thought.

For the rest of their lives.

Epilogue

The wedding was beautiful, exactly as Tommy and Sophie had planned it. She loved every moment of it. For now, they were at the reception, mingling with their guests inside the mansion.

They'd exchanged vows in the garden, beneath a billowy tent, with the jeweled tiger standing guard. She wore a long silk white dress, similar to the gown her mom had worn when she'd wedded Sophie's dad. She definitely felt her parents' presence, like angels from above.

Tommy's family was in full swing. Kirby had walked Sophie down the aisle with pride, and Melinda had lit a glittery gold candle with a romantic scent.

Chance had been a fabulous ring bearer. They'd

decided that Hokey and Pokey could walk with him, and he'd gotten a kick out of the dogs being his loyal companions.

Matt and Libby had done their parts, too. And Brandon. He'd looked exceptional in his tux, standing beside the groom.

Sophie's groom. She glanced across the room at him. At the moment, he was engaged in conversation with a group of their guests.

She placed her hand on her growing belly. Tommy was right about their child. They were having a girl. They hadn't come up with a name for her yet, so they were still calling her Peanut. Sometimes Tommy called her Miss Peanut.

"How's my new sister-in-law?" a voice asked from behind her.

She spun around to meet Brandon's gaze. He'd brought a date to the wedding, one of the socialites he sometimes bedded. But it wasn't serious. It never was with Brandon. His date was off sipping champagne somewhere.

"I'm wonderful," Sophie said. "How are you?"

"I'm doing just fine." He leaned in close, his black hair shining beneath the chandelier above their heads. "This is a smashing event. But Tommy always did know how to throw a party."

"He does have his talents. But so do you." She reached for his hand. "The Talbots wouldn't be the same without you."

"Right." He squeezed her hand. "I'm the one always trying to keep the rest of them out of trouble. But I don't have to worry about Tommy anymore. He's your responsibility now. Then again, I guess he always was. The two of you, like peas in a pod. I should have figured out that you'd get married one day. But I was too busy seeing Tommy for the rebel that he was."

She nodded. "We all were."

"You're the best addition this family could ever have. I'm so glad you and my brother are together now."

"Thank you." She thought about Tommy's hope that Brandon found the love of his life someday. But she wasn't going to say anything about it. She'd already warned Tommy to stay out of Brandon's affairs.

Speaking of her husband, he was making his way over to her. Sophie glanced past Brandon and smiled at her man.

"I think this is my cue to leave." Brandon released her hand. "The groom is enticing his bride."

"He does have that effect on me." As Brandon left, he passed Tommy and patted him on the shoulder.

Eager to be near her husband, Sophie walked straight into his arms. Nothing felt more natural, more glorious, more right.

"This has been the best day of my life so far," she said. She knew they were going to have lots of amazing days.

"Me, too." He kissed her, soft and slow. Then he said, "I wrote a special song for you."

He'd been working on the album inspired by her and the baby, but she assumed this was something she'd yet to hear. "You're going to serenade me?"

He roamed his hands along the fabric-covered buttons marching down the back of her gown. "Yes. But it's a sexy song, so it'll have to wait until we're in bed."

"Mmm." She bumped against him. "A honey-moon song."

"Yep." He circled her waist. "For my naked wife."

"I'm not naked yet." But tonight she would be stripping off her dress for him. The country star she'd just married, the friend and lover who would always have her heart.

* * * * *

Brandon's story is next!

*Look for the third installment of
the Sons of Country series
by Sheri WhiteFeather,
coming March 2019
from
Harlequin Desire.*

COMING NEXT MONTH FROM

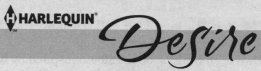

Available December 31, 2018

#2635 THE RANCHER'S BARGAIN

Texas Cattleman's Club: Bachelor Auction
by Joanne Rock

To pay her sister's debt, Lydia Walker agrees to a temporary job as a live-in nanny for hot-as-sin rancher James Harris. There's no denying the magnetic pull between them, but can they untangle their white-hot desire and stubborn differences before time runs out?

#2636 BOMBSHELL FOR THE BOSS

Billionaires and Babies • by Maureen Child

Secretary Sadie Matthews has wanted CEO Ethan Hart for five years—and quitting hasn't changed a thing! But when fate throws him a baby-sized curveball and forces them together again, all the rules are broken and neither can resist temptation any longer...

#2637 THE FORBIDDEN TEXAN

Texas Promises • by Sara Orwig

Despite a century-old family feud, billionaire Texas rancher Jake Ralston hires antiques dealer Emily Kincaid to fulfill a deathbed promise to his friend. But when they're isolated together on his ranch, these enemies' platonic intentions soon become a passion they can't deny...

#2638 THE BILLIONAIRE RENEGADE

Alaskan Oil Barons • by Catherine Mann

Wealthy cowboy Conrad Steele is a known flirt. He's pursued beautiful Felicity Hunt with charm and wit. The spark between them is enough to ignite white-hot desire, but if they're not careful it could burn them both...

#2639 INCONVENIENTLY WED

Marriage at First Sight • by Yvonne Lindsay

Their whirlwind marriage ended quickly, but now both Valentin and Imogene have been matched again—for a blind date at the altar! The passion is still there, but will this second chance mend old wounds, or drive them apart forever?

#2640 AT THE CEO'S PLEASURE

The Stewart Heirs • by Yahrah St. John

Ayden Stewart is a cunningly astute businessman, but ugly family history has him distrustful of love. His gorgeous assistant, Maya Richardson, might be the sole exception—if he can win her back after breaking her heart years ago!

YOU CAN FIND MORE INFORMATION ON UPCOMING HARLEQUIN® TITLES, FREE EXCERPTS AND MORE AT WWW.HARLEQUIN.COM.

HDCNM1218

*Ayden Stewart is a cunningly astute businessman,
but ugly family history has him distrustful of love.
His gorgeous assistant, Maya Richardson, might be
the sole exception—if he can win her back after
breaking her heart years ago!*

Read on for a sneak peek of
At the CEO's Pleasure *by Yahrah St. John,
part of her Stewart Heirs series!*

He would never forget the day, ten years ago, when Maya
Richardson had walked through his door looking for a
job. She'd been a godsend, helping Ayden grow Stewart
Investments into the company it was today. Thinking
of her brought a smile to Ayden's face. How could it
not? Not only was she the best assistant he'd ever had,
Maya had fascinated him. Utterly and completely. Maya
had hidden an exceptional figure beneath professional
clothing and kept her hair in a tight bun. But Ayden had
often wondered what it would be like to throw her over
his desk and muss her up. Five years ago, he hadn't gone
quite that far, but he had crossed a boundary.

Maya had been devastated over her breakup with her
boyfriend. She'd come to him for comfort, and, instead,
Ayden had made love to her. Years of wondering what
it would be like to be with Maya had erupted into a

passionate encounter. Their one night together had been so explosive that the next morning Ayden had needed to take a step back to regain his perspective. He'd had to put up his guard; otherwise, he would have hurt her badly. He thought he'd been doing the right thing, but Maya hadn't thought so. In retrospect, Ayden wished he'd never given in to temptation. But he had, and he'd lost a damn good assistant. Maya had quit, and Ayden hadn't seen or heard from her since.

Shaking his head, Ayden strode to his desk and picked up the phone, dialing the recruiter who'd helped him find Carolyn. He wasn't looking forward to this process. It had taken a long time to find and train Carolyn. Before her, Ayden had dealt with several candidates walking into his office thinking they could ensnare him.

No, he had someone else in mind. A hardworking, dedicated professional who could read his mind without him saying a word and who knew how to handle a situation in his absence. Someone who knew about the big client he'd always wanted to capture but never could attain. She also had a penchant for numbers and research like no one he'd ever seen, not even Carolyn.

Ayden knew exactly who he wanted. He just needed to find out where she'd escaped to.

Don't miss what happens next!
At the CEO's Pleasure *by Yahrah St. John,*
part of her Stewart Heirs series!

Available January 2019 wherever
Harlequin® Desire books and ebooks are sold.

www.Harlequin.com

Love Harlequin romance?

DISCOVER.

Be the first to find out about promotions, news and exclusive content!

f Facebook.com/HarlequinBooks

t Twitter.com/HarlequinBooks

O Instagram.com/HarlequinBooks

P Pinterest.com/HarlequinBooks

ReaderService.com

EXPLORE.

Sign up for the Harlequin e-newsletter and download a free book from any series at **TryHarlequin.com.**

CONNECT.

Join our Harlequin community to share your thoughts and connect with other romance readers!
Facebook.com/groups/HarlequinConnection

HARLEQUIN®

ROMANCE WHEN YOU NEED IT

HSOCIAL2018

THE WORLD IS BETTER WITH

Romance

Harlequin has everything from contemporary, passionate and heartwarming to suspenseful and inspirational stories.

Whatever your mood, we have a romance just for you!

Connect with us to find your next great read, special offers and more.

f/HarlequinBooks

🐦@HarlequinBooks

www.HarlequinBlog.com

www.Harlequin.com/Newsletters

◈HARLEQUIN®

A *Romance* FOR EVERY MOOD™

www.Harlequin.com